# LIFE STUDIES

# LIFE STUDIES

# NANCY GOTTER GATES

**FIVE STAR**
*A part of Gale, Cengage Learning*

GALE
CENGAGE Learning™

Detroit • New York • San Francisco • New Haven, Conn • Waterville, Maine • London

GALE
CENGAGE Learning

LIBRARY OF CONGRESS CATALOGING-IN-PUBLICATION DATA

Gates, Nancy Gotter.
    Life Studies / Nancy Gotter Gates. — 1st ed.
      p. cm.
    ISBN-13: 978-1-4328-2529-4 (hardcover)
    ISBN-10: 1-4328-2529-1 (hardcover)
    1. Widows—Fiction. 2. Middle-aged women—Fiction. 3. Art teachers—Fiction. 4. Life change events—Fiction. I. Title.
    PS3607.A7887L54 2011
    813'.6—dc22                      2011015391

First Edition. First Printing: August 2011.
Published in 2011 in conjunction with Tekno Books.

In memory of my mother and father,
Robert James and Alice Carolyn Gotter

# ACKNOWLEDGMENTS

Thanks to my writing group, Betty DiMeo, Helen Goodman, Lynette Hall Hampton, Harol Marshall and Dorothy P. O'Neill, for their invaluable advice and editing of the manuscript. I also want to thank Greensboro Assistant Chief of Police, Anita Holder, for explaining fraud investigations.

# CHAPTER ONE

She appeared at my door one morning in late spring, slouched back on her heels, hands clasped together in front as if to hide her body, a battered suitcase on the porch beside her. She was an unusual looking young woman; not someone you'd stare at, but perhaps give a second glance to. She didn't smile, just looked at me silently. Her wide-apart eyes were large and rounded with a downward slope accentuated by heavy eyelids. Her dull brown hair pulled back into a ponytail failed to cover ears set low on the head with the lobes tilted in towards the face.

I don't know why, but her hair reminded me of the color of my own before my beautician mercifully colors it auburn, and the ponytail was like the one I wore as a child fifty years ago. Other than that, everything about her was utterly foreign to me.

"Can I help you?" I asked, wondering if she was a homeless person needing a handout.

"I'm looking for Peter Raynor." Her speech was difficult to understand as though her mouth might be slightly deformed.

"I'm sorry, he's not here," I said. I didn't want to go into an explanation about his recent death; I just wanted her to leave. I had laundry piled all over the kitchen floor waiting to be put in the washing machine and the house was in disarray.

"May I come in and wait for him?"

What could I say? I didn't want this strange woman in my house. Why on earth would she want to see Peter? I decided the

9

best way to get rid of her was to tell her the truth. "I'm sorry. Peter died two months ago."

I was unprepared for the torrent of tears my words evoked. She buried her face in her hands and sobbed her heart out. I stood there like a dummy, staring at her. She seemed so distraught that I felt heartless not offering her sympathy.

"Is there anything I can do for you?" I asked.

She shook her head no but continued to cry with her hands over her face. I didn't know what to make of her. I felt I couldn't shut the door in her face when she was so bereft. Finally I said, "Won't you come in for a minute?" I emphasized "minute" hoping she'd take the hint and not stay long.

Finally with a sad nod, she picked up her suitcase and followed me into the living room. I gestured toward the couch and sat in a chair opposite her, waiting for her to calm down. She pulled a handkerchief out of her shoulder bag and wiped the tears away but still said nothing. I got a better look at her now. Her thick neck gave her a round-shouldered look, and her T-shirt and jeans seemed ill fitting. After a moment I realized that her posture, a sunken chest and protruding belly, made her look at first glance like an elderly woman. But now, looking more closely at her, she appeared to be barely in her twenties. As she walked into my house, she came only to my shoulder, and I'm not a tall person, a couple of inches over five feet. I felt a mixture of sympathy and antipathy for this strange woman.

It was an intensely awkward situation. I wanted this person gone, but it seemed she had no intention of leaving soon. I was curious as to why she'd asked for Peter, but at the same time I felt a small frisson of fear. The fact that she had a suitcase and her authentic distress when she learned of his death set off alarm bells in my head.

It was obvious she wasn't going to speak first, so it was up to me. "I'm Liz Raynor. And what is your name?"

With tears still streaming from her eyes, she looked down at her hands folded together in her lap. "I'm Samantha."

A pretty name which didn't suit her at all. "Samantha what?"

"Graves."

It looked as though I would have to pull information out of her bit by bit. I wasn't sure I wanted to do that, but good manners told me I couldn't simply tell her to leave.

"And where are you from, Samantha?"

"Wilmington."

Wilmington is a beautiful seaport town a couple of hundred miles from Greensboro, North Carolina, where I live. It's not too far north of Holden Beach, where Peter and I often spent holidays.

"So why did you come to Greensboro?"

"To find Peter."

How would this young woman from Wilmington know Peter? He had a few clients outside Greensboro who used his services as a financial advisor. He was so admired that when customers moved out of town, they often kept their investments with him, and he would visit them several times a year just to maintain a personal touch. I remembered a couple who used his services had moved to Wilmington some years ago because he made a point of visiting them when we were at the beach. But I'm not sure he ever mentioned their name.

"Was he your financial advisor?" I asked. The thought occurred to me that perhaps some investment he had made for her had tanked and that was why she was so upset. Almost everyone's portfolio had been hit by the recent downturn. Surely she couldn't think he was responsible. On the other hand, her appearance didn't give any indication that this woman ever had much money.

She shook her head no but maintained her silence.

I didn't know what to make of her. I couldn't simply order

11

her out of my house but I was at a loss as to how to handle the situation. Finally, succumbing to the role of hostess I asked her if she wanted something to drink. "Ice tea? Soft drink?"

Finally she looked up at me. "I am thirsty. I'll take a soda."

"Is diet okay? That's all I have."

She nodded.

I was relieved to have an excuse to leave the room and gather myself together. I didn't know how to handle the situation graciously. I had to wonder: if she'd been an attractive, nicely dressed woman would I be having the same reaction?

I brought two drinks back to the living room and handed one to Samantha. I decided it was time to stop equivocating and ask her straight out what she wanted. "If you'd tell me what you wanted to see Peter about, perhaps I could help you."

She stared at me for a couple of minutes before answering. "It's nothing. Never mind."

"But it must have been something," I said, agitated. "You're obviously upset." Nothing drives me crazier than people who beat about the bush and won't tell you what they mean to say.

"It's too late," she said looking completely forlorn.

I wasn't going to play this game with her any more. "Well, then, I have work to do. . . ."

"Can you tell me where I can find a cheap motel?" she interrupted.

From her appearance and her battered suitcase, I wondered if she could afford even a cheap one. "I'm not sure. I'll have to get the telephone directory and check what's out there." The problem was I knew that the cheap ones were probably not that safe.

"How long are you planning to stay in town?"

"Until I decide what to do."

That sounded problematic. "Do you want one with a weekly rate? That would be cheaper in the long run if you're staying a

12

while." There was one not far up Summit Avenue that had been there for years, and I thought it was a reasonably safe place to stay.

When I described it to her she said, "That might be good. Where is it?"

"Right up Summit Avenue, the next street over." I pointed in the direction of the main thoroughfare.

"Okay," she said, getting up from the sofa and picking up her suitcase.

I recalled that I hadn't seen a car when she'd knocked on my door. "How are you going to get there?"

"Walk, of course." She said it matter-of-factly as if she walked everywhere, and it was the accepted mode of transportation. I had to wonder how she got to my house, probably by city bus from the Greyhound depot downtown. I couldn't imagine she had the wherewithal to fly.

I knew I'd not been very hospitable, and I was beginning to feel ashamed. "Let me take you," I said in an attempt to absolve my conscience.

No gracious demurring on her part. "Okay."

She followed me out to the garage and got into my car. The trip took only ten minutes but she didn't say a word. I felt tongue-tied myself. Trying to have a conversation with Samantha was like throwing a ten pound rock into a lake and hoping it would float.

I let her out beside the office door. She muttered "thanks," got her suitcase out of the backseat and disappeared inside. I drove home slowly, trying to come to terms with the emotions Samantha had aroused in me. I simply didn't know what to make of her. What was her connection to Peter and why had she been so devastated by his death?

Peter had always been a kind-hearted man. He belonged to some civic groups and one of them worked with the local Special

Olympics games. I knew that he had been especially touched by the participants and occasionally invited two or three he had come to know to attend baseball games with him. I'm not into baseball, so I had never gone, nor do I remember him ever mentioning the name Samantha. But that didn't mean she wasn't one of those he entertained. I wasn't even sure she was mentally challenged. Perhaps it was her quietness, her refusal to chatter away as most of us do to explain ourselves. But she kept her counsel, unwilling to share with me even though it meant that I couldn't help her. I had to put her out of my mind and consider it case closed.

# CHAPTER TWO

Two months earlier, my husband had passed away after seven months of grueling treatment for acute myelogenous leukemia. In his first hospital stay, hours of toxic chemicals draining into his veins had nearly killed him when he developed pneumonia because his resistance was so low. But that time he survived, went into remission after eight weeks, and was able to come home.

The three months he was home was a quiet time for us, punctuated by overnight trips to the hospital for more chemo. Since he had little immunity, we didn't go out much and mostly read or watched TV. We occasionally had close friends over and pretended life was normal.

One day he went to the hospital for a routine checkup.

"Peter," the doctor said, "the nurses and I are going to have to put up with you a little longer I guess. It's just that your white count and platelets are low. They probably haven't bounced back yet from the last chemo. But we want to keep an eye on you for a few days until it improves."

For once Peter didn't have anything funny to say. He'd always traded jokes with the doctor, but this time he was silent.

As we walked toward the admitting office he said, "I'm never going to leave this place, you know."

"Don't be silly. Of course you are," I answered. I nearly choked on the words.

And he was right. During the last eight weeks of his life I

watched him slowly slip away from me until at the end he was in a coma and didn't respond. Isn't it odd after all the pain and suffering how death arrives so stealthily that if I hadn't been warned of its approach by the doctors, I could almost have believed he was simply having a bad dream?

And so I was alone at age fifty-five after thirty-four years of marriage. In today's world that is young; isn't fifty-five the new forty? I didn't feel forty. I felt ancient. I'd been sleeping on a cot in his room at the hospital for the last eight weeks because my normally brave Peter was afraid to be alone. His fear had seeped into my veins, eroding my confidence and stealing my optimism.

When I returned home, I couldn't stand the thought of sleeping in our king-sized four poster bed by myself, so I sold it and bought a simple double bed. I also sold the recliner that he'd spent so much time in as he recovered from chemotherapy. One represented too many good memories; the other too many bad.

And now I needed to decide what to do with the rest of my life. It seemed to stretch out before me like a long, barren road without road signs to guide me, no global positioning system to show me where to go.

I'd been working in the office of a jewelry store, but I quit when we learned of Peter's grave illness. I didn't want to go back to a job as dull and mundane as that. I could tolerate it when I had another life beyond the office, but that had been buried with my husband. I wanted something that could reenergize me, give me a reason to want to move on. Peter had left me in a position financially to take my time to decide what direction I should go.

"So, now what, Liz?" asked Meredith McKinney, my best friend. We were eating lunch at Panera on Lawndale a month after the funeral.

"I'm not sure," I said. "I'm still trying to settle the estate. I spent what seemed like hours yesterday on the phone with various agencies trying to get things straightened out. It seems like they throw up a roadblock at every turn just to frustrate you. What happens with little old ladies who are unable to deal with the red tape when their husbands die?"

"They'd better have someone who can handle it for them. I think someone should start an agency called 'Help for the Harassed,' but it would take a saint to be able to deal with all the machinations of the bureaucracy. I almost lost my mind over my mother's estate." Considering her background, that surprised me. Meredith is a patent lawyer, one of a handful in Greensboro. She is brilliant and holds degrees in computer science as well as law, though her personal life is a train wreck. She's forty-nine but looks at least ten years younger with shoulder-length blond hair (thanks to her hairdresser), a trim figure and beautiful clothes. Married and divorced three times, I think she's finally decided that she's not marriage material. At least this week. Next week could be a whole other story.

In fact, although Peter had been gone for only a month, I was somewhat surprised that Meredith hadn't yet urged me to check out eHarmony. She has always been a bit amazed, and I think secretly envious, that Peter and I had stuck it out for thirty-four years.

When I say "stuck it out" it sounds as though our married life was a battlefield, which is not true. We certainly didn't have a perfect marriage—is there such a thing?—but we learned early on how to deal with our differences in a pretty low key, non-confrontational way, and I'd say we had one of the better relationships of all the married couples I know.

The one sour note was the fact that I badly wanted children but was unable to have them. For the first few years of our marriage I became severely depressed each month when I found I wasn't pregnant. After several years of futility, we learned Peter carried a gene that could cause severe birth defects in his offspring, and so we placated ourselves with the fact that it was probably just as well I never conceived.

We once had a discussion about adoption, but our hearts weren't in it. We had wanted our own child, our own flesh and blood, and when that wasn't possible, we simply resigned ourselves to our childless state and made enhancing our relationship our number one priority.

"Do you need to work?" Meredith sucked noisily on her straw trying for the last few drops of tea she could retrieve. She'd already finished her French onion soup and half of a tuna salad sandwich while I was still working on my cream of chicken with wild rice soup. My appetite was still not back to normal, probably stunted by the awful hospital meals I'd endured for eight weeks.

I wasn't surprised by her question, which might be considered a little gauche. She and I had always been open with one another on almost every subject except money. I'm not sure why. I felt more comfortable discussing sex than I did our income. Perhaps that was a result of my upbringing when finances were discussed between my parents only after the children were in bed. My sister and I had no idea how much money our father made until after he died. We were shocked to discover he'd saved a considerable sum even though he was employed as a teacher all his life. But we had always lived a very frugal existence. I'm sure my parents were influenced by the Great Depression and saved their money against any similar events in the future. That inheritance as well as what I received from Peter's insurance and investments made it possible for me to live comfortably the rest of my life without additional income.

"I'm fine, financially speaking," I said, not willing to be any more specific than that. "But when you ask do I *need* to work, the answer is yes. I need to find something to engage me. I don't want to go back to what I was doing before. I only did that to get out of the house. But now that I'm alone, I need to find something that's fulfilling."

"Like what?"

"You got me there, Meredith. I don't have a clue."

"How about volunteer work?" Meredith was deeply involved with the movers and shakers in the city on big-time fundraising events that attracted the wealthy who wanted to be seen in all the right places. That didn't appeal to me. I'd never felt comfortable at cocktail parties where I had to make small talk with people I didn't know and didn't particularly care about. And Peter, who had his own investment business, never liked big social events either. We had a small circle of friends which suited us just fine.

The thing was, and I'd never admit this to Meredith, that I hadn't heard much from my married friends since Peter's funeral. I'd heard this could happen. Women are nervous that newly-widowed friends might make moves on their husbands, but there wasn't a husband in our group that I would ever be interested in romantically. They were nice guys; we had enjoyed getting together with them as a couple. But I always secretly felt that Peter was head and shoulders above the rest of them. I wasn't being snobbish, just sure that he was more intelligent, talented, and, yes, better looking than the other men in our crowd.

"I used to deliver Meals on Wheels once a month before Peter became ill. I felt good about that though I admit I wasn't going to receive any volunteer awards for my meager involvement. But I need to do something to get my creative juices flowing again. That's what sustains me."

"Then why don't you buy another house that needs fixing

up? I've never seen you happier than when you were doing that."

Although we could have afforded to live in a large house in one of the upscale neighborhoods of Greensboro, Peter and I had agreed that we didn't want more space or yard than we could comfortably take care of ourselves. Since there were just the two of us and we both worked, that meant a small craftsman house in the Aycock neighborhood, a historic area off Summit Avenue, not far from downtown. It had been something of a wreck when we first saw it fifteen years ago, but we slowly brought it back to its original glory with a lot of hard labor and loving care. Maybe I used the restoration of the house as a substitute for raising children, but it satisfied my need to be nurturing and creative. I spent many hours scraping paint, sanding wood, painting walls, and laying tile while Peter did the heavy stuff like remodeling the kitchen. We had to hire professional plumbers and electricians, but we did all the rest of the work.

The house had become such an expression of us as a couple that I felt I could never sell it. It was almost like a third party to our marriage. The essence of Peter was everywhere.

"I don't think so," I said. "I certainly don't want anything bigger now that I'm alone, and to get any smaller I'd probably have to go to a condo. And I don't want to do that."

"If you don't want a fixer upper, the advantage of a condo is that it's maintenance free. You wouldn't have to worry about the yard work or keeping things up." Meredith lived in one of those pricey condos in Grandover that were as large as or larger than many single homes.

"I can tend what little yard I have, and I'll hire someone when it comes to big jobs like painting the house. I love my historic neighborhood. At least I can walk to the store which is more than you can do."

Meredith sighed and rattled the ice in her glass before tipping it to her mouth for any lingering drops of tea before speaking. "You're incorrigible, Liz. No matter what I suggest, you turn it down. I hope you're not going to turn into a recluse."

I laughed. "No way. I'm not the social butterfly that you are, never have been. But I'm not going to hide away with the blinds drawn. I'll think of something."

"I sincerely hope so. I worry about you. You're not the fun person you used to be."

"My god, Meredith. It's only been a month. Give me time!"

She wasn't really being disrespectful. It's just that she could bounce from one relationship to the next without being unduly hurt emotionally. I don't think she ever cared deeply enough about any of her partners to suffer much when they parted. She didn't know what it meant to have a vital, lasting connection with someone.

It might seem strange that we were such good friends considering how different we were. But they say opposites attract, and her qualities of self-confidence, outgoing personality, and sense of humor were endearing. She had so many traits I lacked that I suppose I hoped they would somehow rub off on me.

Meredith returned to work, and I ran a few errands before returning home. It was still a shock for me to open the door to an empty house. Peter often got home before I did because his office was closer, and the enticing aromas of the meal he was preparing would greet me when I arrived. I felt that I'd won the lottery when I learned that Peter loved to cook because I always found it an onerous chore. My mother was a pretty fair cook, but she never had the patience to teach my sister Gwen and me. So I never learned to do much more than flip burgers and microwave frozen dinners. When Peter remodeled the kitchen, he filled it with the best appliances he could find: a six-burner

21

gas stove, a capacious refrigerator, and high end pots and pans.

Now I was just as likely to make a peanut butter and jelly sandwich or order a pizza than try to put together a decent meal. I knew I had to start eating better before I came down with malnutrition or scurvy.

Such a sense of emptiness swept over me it almost brought me to my knees. At first the loneliness engulfed me like a shroud. It was stifling and unrelenting. Now it came and went in waves. When I was busy, I could stave it off for a while, but when there was a break from settling the estate or every day chores like grocery shopping or cleaning, the realization that Peter was gone forever hit me like a physical blow.

I sat down and wept at the thought of the long empty future that awaited me.

# CHAPTER THREE

A couple of days later the weather, in typical Greensboro style, turned from chilly gloom to splendid sunshine and warmth. April can mimic almost any season of the year, but it was clothed in all its spring glory that day. I decided to walk down to Wendy's on Summit Avenue for a double stack and a Frosty. I live on Fifth Avenue near Yanceyville Street, just a few blocks away. Spring is dazzling in our town with its wealth of Bradford pear trees, dogwood and redbud in prolific bloom overhead and yards ablaze with azaleas of every hue. Color is everywhere, luxuriant and soul satisfying. I always want to bottle it up to save for the dreary days of winter.

As I rounded the corner of Yanceyville onto Summit, I caught a glimpse of the Sternberger Artists' Center on the far side of the street. A large brick Mediterranean-inspired home built for the Sternberger family in the nineteen twenties, it served as a center for artists and writers for a number of years. I've walked or driven by it almost daily but never gave it much thought.

This time, however, I couldn't help but stop and stare. A rectangular brick home topped by a green tile roof, with an inset entrance enhanced by three arches supported by Corinthian columns, it's a remnant of the once stately homes that lined this street in the early part of the twentieth century. With the exception of a few large homes converted to offices, most had been torn down to make way for nondescript insurance offices and other small businesses. Just up the street at the corner of Bessemer and Summit is the first strip shopping center built in town.

But the Sternberger house has been preserved in all its glory, thanks in part to being named to the National Register of Historic Places. A sweeping green lawn leads up to the wide tile-surfaced front porch, and its windows give glimpses into its restored interior.

I don't know why I hadn't thought of it before. I'd been playing around at drawing and painting all of my life. When I went to college I considered majoring in art, but when I learned that the emphasis was on abstract painting, I lost interest. I love drawing the human form, especially children. It seems to me that all children are so beautiful, so natural, that they have always been my favorite subject. This made it all the more difficult to accept the fact I could never have any of my own.

Seeing the Sternberger house made me realize that I could now paint to my heart's content, though I had much to learn. I'd taken a lesson here and there but had made no concentrated effort at studying art. It occurred to me that if I could rent a studio at the artists' center, I wouldn't have interruptions and I could leave my easel and paints out. Our little house had only two bedrooms, one of which served as a guest room, so space to spread out and immerse myself in my work didn't exist.

After eating at Wendy's I hurried home to get my car and drove downtown to the offices of the United Arts Council which owned the property, to see if any studios were available. To my delight, I was told that a studio was being vacated the very next week.

I called Meredith that night, filled with excitement.

"I think I found what I was looking for," I said when she answered.

"What? A new spring dress or did you find some cute shoes?" she asked.

"Do you ever think about anything but clothes?"

"How about men?"

"You're impossible," I said. "No, I told you the other day I needed to decide what to do with the rest of my life."

"Oh, *that!*" she said with a laugh. "Of course I do. I was just giving you a hard time."

"Well, at least I have a start on it. I'm renting a studio at the Sternberger Arts Center."

"You mean that big brick house on Summit?"

"Yes. A room is opening up next week. And I'm told it's the best one in the building. It was the library." I was pacing the living room as I talked to her, mentally going over the art supplies I would need.

"So you're going to sit over there and read?"

"I'm going to paint."

"Oh. That's nice," she said, with little enthusiasm.

"You know I've dabbled in it off and on for years."

"Well, sure. But I never thought you took it seriously."

I'd never showed any of my work to Meredith because I wasn't especially proud of it. And I knew she wouldn't be complimentary just to spare my feelings. If nothing else, she's honest, sometimes to the point of being hurtful. But I'd long ago shrugged it off. Whenever she says something unkind I always think *that's just her way.* And I never let it get to me. But as far as my art work was concerned, my ego was much too fragile to subject it to her frankness.

"I just thought it was a good time to see if I have any talent. I know I've got a lot to learn, but it's something that's always given me a lot of pleasure. If it doesn't work out, it doesn't work out."

"That's true. All you've wasted is a few dollars on paints and brushes."

"Right," I answered, thinking *thanks for the encouragement.*

I hadn't painted since Peter got sick, so I went through my art supplies to see what I needed to replenish. Some of my watercolor tubes had hardened to the point where I couldn't get the lids off or squeeze out any paint so I made a list of the colors I needed: yellow ochre, cadmium yellow, cadmium red, alizarin crimson, burnt sienna, shades I would use to paint flesh colors. I was also out of Hooker's green and ultramarine blue as well as some 300-pound hot press watercolor paper which has a smooth finish. Cold press paper, which many artists use, has a rougher finish. But I don't think I'm adept enough to handle it well. My brushes were adequate for the time being. I wanted to buy expensive Kolinsky sable brushes, but I didn't want to make the investment until I was sure that I was going to persevere in my hobby.

Even though I couldn't get into the studio for several days, I couldn't wait to buy my supplies, so I drove out to the art and craft supply store on New Garden Road. When I gathered up the tubes of paint in a carrying basket, I felt as though I were harvesting a crop of hopes and dreams. Could I ever do something magical with them? Could I take my meager talent and grow it like those who have developed a green thumb grow beautiful flowers in their garden?

I threw in a kneaded eraser, some tracing paper, and a box of drawing pencils for good measure.

When I got home I packed all of my art materials in several boxes and stored them in the guest room. I didn't want to waste a minute once I could get into the studio the following week.

# CHAPTER FOUR

The following Wednesday turned out to be another bright and beautiful day. I'd picked up the keys the day before, so I loaded the boxes of art supplies into the trunk of my car and drove to the studio.

I pulled around to the paved back yard of the artists' center and parked against the hedge that separated it from the squat white brick building to the south that was currently empty. A For Lease sign in the yard was typical of the economic downturn that had closed many businesses in town. I let myself in the rear door and went to the first room on the left. Unlocking the door, I was greeted with abundant sunshine flooding the room from the two large windows overlooking the parking lot. They didn't face north, which would have been ideal, but east which meant abundant morning light. Since I'm a morning person and would probably use the studio early in the day, that was fine with me. The opposite wall contained ceiling-high bookcases. It would be a perfect place to store my supplies and art books. There was a door on the far wall which opened into a large living room that ran from the front to the back of the house. At the rear, a small solarium brought light to a huge display of Boston ferns on a tile ledge under the windows. A large fireplace with a carved mantel graced the long wall of the living room which was furnished with a lengthy antique table and chairs. At the center front of the house, a large foyer, its walnut paneling adding to the gracious ambience, showcased the stairway to the second floor. I knew I was going to love it here.

I took the better part of the morning putting away all my supplies and books. The shelves were a blessing because I'd collected so many art books over the years I had to store them in the attic. Both Peter and I devoured books—I preferred fiction and he nonfiction—and they filled what bookcases we had. I belonged to one of those book clubs that caters to artists and in almost every catalog I found at least one book that I would be enticed to buy, sure that it would help transform me into an accomplished artist, even though I had nowhere to keep it out where I could use it. Now I would have a chance to read through all of them at my leisure.

The previous tenant had left a big old oak desk behind. I was delighted because I'd planned to go to a used furniture store to buy an old table. Though I stand in front of an easel when I paint with acrylics, I sit down with a board propped on a table when I use watercolors so they won't run down the page, and the old desk would serve the purpose. There was a tiny lavatory next to my studio so a water source was convenient.

Once everything was put away, I wandered to the second floor which I hadn't yet explored. Apparently no one else was in the building at this hour and since all the doors were closed, there wasn't much to see. The woman at United Arts Council had told me that many of the tenants worked there at night because they had daytime jobs.

I had an appointment about the estate with my lawyer, so I couldn't stay to paint. But I was anxious to return and begin the first day of the rest of my life. I knew the pain of losing Peter would never go away, but I hoped that immersing myself in something I loved would help ease the ache inside me.

The next morning I decided dirty clothes be damned. Instead of doing laundry I'd go to the studio for a little while. I'd have to rethink my priorities: do housework or paint. Now that I was alone, I could live with some clutter and dust.

A blue sedan was parked behind the center, and I was excited at the prospect of meeting another tenant. I let myself in and saw that the door was open to a space I assumed had originally been the dining room on the opposite side of the foyer from the living room. The open door seemed like an invitation, so I went quietly over to peek in, not wanting to disturb its occupant. The room was large with an elaborate chandelier hanging from the center of the ceiling. It was nearly empty except for a woman seated at a makeshift desk made of two low filing cabinets with a board across the top. She was younger than I, I would guess in her forties, with straight brown hair that hung well below her shoulders, and she wore faded jeans and a UNCG T-shirt. She was bent over the table writing on a legal pad. An old portable typewriter and a ream of paper were the only other items on the desktop.

She was so absorbed in what she was doing I didn't want to disturb her. She seemed to sense I was standing there and turned around.

"Oh, hi," she said, pushing back her chair and standing. "You must be our new neighbor. I'm Rachel Levine."

I stepped into the room and shook her hand.

"Liz Raynor. You must be a writer."

"A short story writer," she said. "And a fool, I guess, since there is very little market for short stories these days. Besides, I'm a throwback to the dinosaur age. I don't use a computer."

"Well, I paint, but strictly for my own enjoyment. I certainly couldn't sell anything. I'm just a novice."

"Well, we should form a little society then. Those of us here who do our thing merely for the love of it."

"Would there be many in our group?" I asked.

"Probably just the two of us. Everyone else teaches or has an outside job to help support themselves, but they've all reached a pretty high level of competence. A couple of writers have sold their books to New York publishers, and the artists have work in a number of galleries. So I'm glad to have a neighbor like me. I've been feeling very outclassed."

"Then having me here should make you feel better," I said. "Maybe we can cheer each other on."

"I'd love that."

I didn't want to interrupt her work any longer, but I did want to get to know her better. "Would you be interested in going out to lunch later?" I asked.

"Sure," she said. And we made arrangements to go to the nearby Café Europa.

I was excited at the prospect of making a new friend, especially since my married friends had fallen by the wayside now that Peter was gone. I had no idea if Rachel was married or not, but at least we could see each other at the center and discuss our passions. Peter encouraged me to paint but he had no real interest in it, so I'd never had anyone to share my enthusiasm. Meredith always thought of it as child's play. Although Rachel wasn't an artist, as creative people we could share some common ground.

Back in my studio, I searched through boxes of photos I'd saved over the years looking for a subject to paint. I found a snapshot I liked of a young girl digging in the sand at Holden beach and began to sketch it on tracing paper first to keep from having to do a lot of erasing on the watercolor paper. Before I knew it, it was quarter to twelve.

Rachel knocked on the open door to announce herself. "Ready?"

I drove my car to the parking deck on Church Street and we got to Café Europa early, so there was no problem getting a table on the patio. The sun was warm though a breeze kept it comfortable. We each ordered a glass of ice tea and a salad.

"So how long have you been at Sternberger?" I asked.

"Almost two years," Rachel said. "I started upstairs in what amounts to a closet in the front. A stained glass artist was in the room I'm in now. He left a couple of months ago, and I moved in. The little place upstairs was cozy but it was hot as hell in the summer."

"So who's in there now?"

"I haven't met her yet. But I think she's a poet. So tell me about yourself, Liz."

Reluctantly I told her about Peter's illness and death as briefly as possible. "I'm trying to restart my life, find something to be passionate about," I told her. "His death seems to have taken away everything I cared for. I know it's trite to say you feel like an empty shell, but that's the best way I know how to express it."

"Well at least you're making the effort to reinvent yourself. That's so much better than sitting around bemoaning your fate. You're still young, and you have a full life ahead of you."

"I hope so. In so many ways I feel that it's over. But I can't think like that. I'm fighting my depression as hard as I can." I amazed myself by being so frank with Rachel whom I barely knew. While I hadn't felt comfortable confessing my true feelings to Meredith, my friend of many years, here I was unloading my soul on this poor woman. But something about her invited one to share confidences. It was a healing experience.

Rachel didn't say anything for a few minutes as she watched the traffic on Davie Street. Then she turned back to me and said, "My story is I'm recently divorced. That's like experiencing a death, but in some ways I think it's worse."

How could anything be worse I thought. It must have shown on my face because Rachel, after hesitating, went on. "It's worse because you know that you have failed somehow. In a good marriage, when a partner dies, you grieve, but you have good memories to cherish. In a divorce, only bitterness remains."

She looked so sad that I reached across the table and put my hand on top of hers. "I see what you mean," I said. "I hadn't thought about it that way."

Rachel told me pretty much the story of her life as we lingered over our lunch. She was originally from upstate New York but had come here to attend the University of North Carolina at Greensboro. She met her ex-husband in a class there, and they wed as soon as they graduated. They were married for fifteen years which meant she was in her mid-thirties. She'd had a series of miscarriages which had led to depression.

"I'm not surprised John left me," she said as her eyes teared up. "I was hell on wheels for a number of years. I didn't go to a therapist until after he left, so I guess I have only myself to blame. I kept thinking I could beat it by myself."

"I've been there," I said. "Only I couldn't get pregnant at all. I used to sit and bawl all day every time I had a period."

"Your husband must have been more understanding."

"He was." I couldn't help but smile. "He'd bring me a little gift each time to cheer me up. After several years, we just decided to give up."

"Well, John found another woman who could have babies and decided he'd rather be with her." Rachel put her fork down as she struggled to get her emotions under control.

I realized that she had as much to mourn as I did.

When she regained her composure, she told me she had received enough money from the divorce that she didn't have to work if she watched her pennies. John was a big-time contractor in the area, and they had lived in Irving Park, the most prestigious address in Greensboro. She now lived in one of the new condos that had been built along Elm Street in the downtown area.

"I live in the Aycock neighborhood," I told her, "just around the corner from Sternberger. I'm close enough to downtown without having to put up with the noise and crowds on the weekends."

"That's what gives it its ambience," she said.

"Wait till you're my age. You might prefer peace and quiet."

This made her smile. "Oh, come on. That sounds like you're ready for the retirement center."

"No, no. Just because I like a low key life doesn't mean I'm over the hill."

"Well, maybe each of us should stick our toe in the waters of the dating scene. It's easier, I think, when you try it with a friend."

"I'm nowhere near ready for that," I said. "Maybe men can jump right in again after losing their wives, but I haven't begun to process my grief."

Rachel looked stricken as though she'd said something terrible. "I'm so sorry," she said, "I was only trying to. . . ."

"Don't apologize. I know you meant well. One of these days I might consider it," I said, doubting very much that it would happen anytime soon.

# CHAPTER FIVE

I found solace and comfort in my space at Sternberger. I went there nearly every morning and worked until at least noon, sometimes well into the afternoon. I bought a small dorm-size refrigerator and microwave so I could keep frozen meals if I stayed past lunchtime. About once a week I went out to lunch with Rachel, and I was becoming quite fond of her.

About two weeks after I started painting there, I had dinner with Meredith at Green Valley Grill, one of our favorite restaurants.

"So how is the art studio working out?" she asked once we'd ordered our meals. We both chose the roast butternut squash couscous.

"Pretty well. I get so absorbed in painting I almost forget how lonely I am."

"Which brings up a point I wanted to make with you. I'm dating a new guy now."

She looked very pleased with herself as she buttered her bread.

Did that surprise me? Meredith wasn't happy unless there was a man in her life. "That's nice," I said hoping I sounded more enthusiastic than I felt.

"Bill has a single friend who's available. How about double dating with us?"

I couldn't imagine anything that appealed to me less. Meredith's choice of men was less than stellar, and I knew any friend of one of her boyfriends would *not* be someone who would appeal to me. "Thanks, Meredith," I said. "But I'm far from being ready to do that."

"You're not getting any younger, Liz," she said sternly. "You can't wait forever."

"People remarry in their eighties these days. What are you talking about? I have all the time in the world." I crammed a piece of bread in my mouth before I said something I'd regret.

"Are you planning on waiting another thirty years?" Her tone reminded me of my mother's when I'd done something to displease her.

"Of course not," I snapped. "It's only been six weeks, Meredith. Give me a break."

She gave me a weak smile. "I'm sorry, Liz. I didn't mean to upset you. I just want you to be happy."

"Me, too. Only it doesn't take a man in my life to do that, you know." After I said it, I realized Meredith might misconstrue my remark and take it as a slap in the face. But I shouldn't have worried. It went right past her.

She looked at me quizzically. "Don't be so sure."

Why couldn't Meredith—and Rachel for that matter—just leave me alone, for heaven's sake? They acted like there was something innately wrong with being a single woman. I knew I shouldn't have been upset with Meredith. But even after I got home, her words stuck in my mind. I couldn't even begin to think about another man yet. My sense of loss was still too raw. Peter had been a part of my life for so long that I couldn't envision anyone else taking his place.

Meredith had asked me whether I wanted to be alone for the next thirty years. It was a question I couldn't deal with yet. I was going to take my life one step at a time and see where it led me. That's all I was capable of doing.

★ ★ ★ ★ ★

It was a couple of weeks later when the doorbell rang shortly after two in the afternoon. I'd been in my studio painting all morning and had come home reluctantly because I knew if I didn't do a load of wash, I wouldn't have a thing to wear. My dirty laundry was sorted into piles on the floor of the kitchen and the rest of the house wasn't in very good shape either. The more time I spent at Sternberger, the less time I spent picking up and vacuuming and dusting, chores I heartily disliked. I excused my lapses by telling myself that tending the flame of creativity was more important than a clean house. But now the thought of someone seeing the mess made me embarrassed. I hoped that it was a salesman or someone I could turn away. I didn't want to invite anyone to come inside and see my slovenliness. But my housekeeping turned out to be the least of my worries.

The visitor turned out to be Samantha when she came to ask about Peter. After dropping her off at the motel, my mind wouldn't leave the subject alone. Who was this woman? What was her relationship to Peter? After talking with her that day, I didn't really believe he'd met her through Special Olympics. As odd looking as she appeared and as little as she had to say, I got the impression she was not mentally challenged. I tried as hard as I could to convince myself that the connection was through her family who must have been clients. And she had come to talk to him because they'd lost their savings in the market crash. I didn't dare let myself explore other options. Whatever the reason, I felt there was nothing I could do to right whatever wrong had befallen her. It wasn't my business.

I was having lunch with Meredith the following week when I told her about Samantha.

"Talk about a 'riddle wrapped in a mystery inside an

enigma,' " I said. "I couldn't make heads nor tails of the woman. She knew Peter from somewhere but she wouldn't tell me where."

"Well, I wouldn't sweat it then," Meredith said. "From your description, it sounds like she was looking for a handout."

"No, she didn't ask for a thing. She was even going to walk to the motel until I told her I'd take her."

"Be thankful. She could have made up some story about how Peter cheated her out of money. She probably broke down when she realized her scam wasn't going to work since Peter had died."

"Good lord, Meredith, what a curmudgeon you have turned into."

"Hey, with the economy the way it is, scam artists are coming out of the woodwork. You have to watch your backside at all times."

I had questioned Samantha's motives, but I couldn't quite envision her doing anything like that. Meredith had become so skeptical of everybody's intentions these days that she was downright peevish. I was relieved that Peter had not been *her* financial advisor. She probably would have blamed him for the beating her portfolio had taken. If that had been the case, I know our friendship could not have survived. As it was, her negative attitude was taking a toll on it.

"Let's change the subject," I said. "How's your love life these days?" I really didn't want to hear about it, but it was the only way I knew to distract her.

Meredith smiled for the first time since we began eating. "Ah, Bill. What a guy! He's so romantic, Liz. He sends me flowers all the time, calls me several times a day."

My heart did a little flutter. Peter had been romantic, too. He used to leave little love notes around the house where I'd find them while doing my daily chores. He'd call me from his office at least once a day to tell me how much he loved me. I missed those little gestures so much. It was like someone ordering you to stay off all sweets when you have a raging sweet tooth. *He loved me so much that there was simply no question that he was faithful.*

"That's great, Meredith," I said, though in my heart I'd wished she hadn't told me that. I didn't want my thoughts to go off on disquieting tangents.

"He still wants to fix you up with his friend."

"Tell him thanks, but I'm not ready yet."

"Okay then," Meredith said, shaking her head in dismay, "I won't mention it again. *You* tell *me* when you're ready to go out. I'll try to help you out—if there are any single guys around by then."

The days went by smoothly, blending into each other. The summer was unusually hot but I had a window air conditioner aided by a floor fan in my studio that made the room reasonably comfortable. I spent nearly every morning at Sternberger, and if I was really caught up in a painting, sometimes part or all of the afternoon. I could see that I was making slow progress. I still had a long way to go, but the daily practice was helping me understand all the nuances of working in watercolor, a particularly tricky medium. I would hang my pictures on the walls of the room with painters' tape and study them, trying to figure out how to improve my use of color and particularly enhance the contrast between dark and light.

At first my paintings seemed rather flat because I hadn't mastered the use of chiaroscuro, the contrast between shadow and light. But I was slowly learning to by simply trying over and over again. I had gone from painting exclusively from photos of children on the beach to setting up still lifes with bowls and candlesticks and other items from my home along with fruit and vegetables. Since the farmers' market was around the corner from my studio, I bought plump ripe tomatoes and fat yellow onions, various kinds of colorful squash and gourds to create a scene. Because I bought so much fresh produce, I was learning to cook new recipes from the leftover props. And I was enjoying it, much to my surprise. I guess I'd been lazy since Peter had been so willing to do the cooking. But I was learning there can be a great deal of creativity in preparing a meal.

I couldn't get Samantha out of my thoughts. A couple of times I drove by the motel wondering if I could catch sight of her. Of course, even if I did, I had no idea what I would do about it. Once, as I was walking down the driveway from my studio on my way home, I thought I saw her about a block away with her back towards me. I rushed after her, only to discover it was an elderly woman walking to the fast food place on the corner. Luckily I was able to see her profile before I reached her. The woman probably would have thought I'd lost my mind.

Rachel and I continued to have lunch together about once a week. Even though I was old enough to be her mother, she was so mature and comfortable in her own skin that it didn't feel as if there was any age difference at all. And we were both working through our frustrations and roadblocks when it came to our goals. Rachel had to deal with rejection at a higher level than I did because she received standard form letters from editors with vague sentences saying something like "sorry, not for us," without explaining *why* her story didn't suit them. I could always tell when she'd gotten one of those awful letters. She'd be quieter than normal and not as cheery.

I, on the other hand, was my own worst critic. I knew that my paintings fell well short of my expectations, but I had trouble putting my finger on what went wrong.

One day at lunch Rachel told me she was joining a local writers' group. "I've been trying too long to go it alone. It's impossible to be objective about my own writing. I always thought mine was too advanced to need a group to pass judgment on it, but I know now that was a big mistake. I need feedback from other writers who are experiencing what I'm going through."

"Well, if nothing else you all can commiserate with each other when you get rejected. They must be struggling as much as you are, and it helps to know you're not alone when you get one of those awful letters."

"Right. It's like a support group for any addict. We just happen to be addicted to writing. Maybe I'll learn the twelve steps to success." She laughed.

"If it were only that simple," I said. "I struggle every day. I guess I should look for a support group, too."

As I lay in bed that night, I thought again about our conversation. I was only making small talk when I said I should look for a support group. But the more I thought about it, the more sense it made. Why continually make the same mistakes over and over through ignorance when I could take a class and learn proper techniques? I resolved to look into it the next day.

Instead of going to my studio the next morning, I went downtown to the Cultural Arts Center because I knew they offered various art classes for children and adults. I found that the Art Alliance offered a life studies class on painting the human figure. I'd never tried to paint anything but children, but I thought it would be a good learning experience to paint adults. I'd learn about anatomy as well as how to use color effectively. The life studies class didn't start until October, several weeks away, but I signed up to ensure a place in it.

The evening the class started, I arrived with a large pad of newsprint, charcoal sticks, and drawing pencils as the supply list had specified. I felt nervous, anxious at the idea of having my drawings seen by a group of people who were probably far more advanced than I was. No one but Peter had ever seen any of my work, and he offered no comment. He'd say he was no art critic and couldn't judge.

"But you could offer an opinion," I said to him.

"No, I don't have the expertise; but if it makes you happy, I say go for it," he'd tell me.

That didn't exactly give me any confidence. I guess he was afraid if he said the wrong thing, it might discourage me. And he knew he was transparent to me. If he praised my work insincerely, I'd see through it in a minute.

It was a pretty large class, ten women and five men of assorted ages. The others briskly set up easels and laid out their materials as if they'd done it many times before.

The instructor was a man of about sixty. He introduced himself as Julian Kadlacek. "Most people call me Jay Kay," he said. "My last name is hard enough to pronounce and harder yet to spell." He had rugged features, not handsome in the usual sense because his nose was large and his ears stood out a little. His close cropped hair bristled with wiry gray curls. But he had a smile that warmed your heart. In fact I soon learned if he smiled while critiquing my work it took the sting out of his words.

The model the first night was a buxom young woman who apparently had posed for the class before. Everyone greeted her as she slipped into the room in a bathrobe. "Hey, Victoria," they said almost in unison. She was pretty in a Rubenesque way with long auburn hair and skin the color of pale pink marble. I felt a moment of embarrassment as she dropped her robe and reclined on a platform in the middle of the room. I'd never been in the presence of a naked woman in front of several men. But as soon as I picked up my charcoal and began sketching, my discomfort quickly vanished.

The class began with quick five or ten minute sketches as she changed her pose at the sound of a bell that Jay rang. At first I had barely begun drawing when she'd take a new pose. But eventually I learned how to draw quickly, trying to capture the flow of the body and arms and legs with just a few lines. There was no time to put in a lot of detail.

Jay came up behind me while I was feverishly trying to complete a picture. A vague odor of turpentine exuded from his clothing, cargo pants and a T-shirt that both bore streaks of oil paint. I never thought of turpentine as an aphrodisiac, but apparently the intense atmosphere of creativity added to its pungent smell awakened some kind of feeling in me that I thought had disappeared permanently.

He pointed to the model's right arm. "See how her arm is foreshortened? That's always tricky when you're looking straight on at an arm or a leg." He had a pencil in his hand and he held it out at arm's length with the tip pointed up. "See this? The upper part of the arm is this long," he marked the spot on the pencil with his thumbnail to indicate its length. "But the lower arm is only this long." He moved the pencil down to measure the forearm and showed me that this distance, because of the angle of the arm, was only half as long. "You can use the pencil as well to find the distances in the face, from the top of the head to the eyes, where the nose and mouth go, and so on. That's the artist's ruler."

His voice was low and soothing, and he seemed genuinely concerned about what I was doing. No one had ever seemed interested before. Rachel was always kind enough to listen to me go on about my struggles, but so far I'd refused to show her my work. I didn't feel I was ready to show it to anyone. So I felt pretty much like a virgin as far as my art was concerned.

"Nice job," Jay purred. "I can see you have innate talent. Keep up the good work."

I could feel the heat as a blush rose up my face. I was so

unused to praise that it made me almost dizzy. I wasn't sure whether I was reacting to what he said or to him. Perhaps my emotions hadn't suffered from total annihilation after all.

Jay walked on to the next student, seemingly unaware of my reaction. Thank God for that.

By the end of the session we'd done a dozen quick sketches of Victoria. I could see some improvement between my first and last attempts. I found that I had loosened up considerably, a consequence of the brief time we had with each pose. In the past I'd spent long minutes fussing over every line, trying to make it exactly as I saw it. Now I found that the drawing was much more lively when it was done more rapidly, trying to capture the flow of the body. From now on when drawing children or adults, I'd begin with the looseness I'd acquired that evening and then work with that initial impression to finalize the picture.

# CHAPTER SIX

Meredith and I decided to take in a movie together one Sunday a couple of weeks after I'd begun my class. We went to Mimi's at the Shops at Friendly afterward for a light supper.

"What's the latest?" I asked her as we sat in a booth awaiting our salads. She'd been extra busy lately and we hadn't been able to get together for about three weeks.

"Work's about to kill me," she said, stirring artificial sweetener into her tea. "Other lawyers may be having a tough time, but the requests for patent applications still keep rolling in. I guess in the long run that's good for the economy, but frankly I'm about to burn out. That's why I asked you to go to the movie today. I've worked straight through the past three weekends, and I'm not going to do that any more. Besides, it plays hell with my love life."

"Speaking of which," I said, "that was my next question."

Meredith rolled her eyes in disgust. "Bill's long gone. He had no patience with my long work hours. He wanted me to be there for him at his beck and call. *Men!*" she said disgustedly. "They can let you wait to hear from them when they're working late or out with their buddies, but you'd better jump to it when they crook their little finger."

"I'm so sorry, Meredith. You know, it's not the end of the world to be a single woman. As much as I miss Peter, I find that being alone isn't the absolute worst thing that can happen to you. You just have to call upon your own resources to make life pleasant."

Her eyes grew teary. This startled me because Meredith always seemed so in control. "Maybe you have the resources for that. I'm not so sure I do."

I reached over and patted her hand. "Of course you do. You just haven't developed them yet because you've depended on men to make you happy. But so often in the end, they've done the opposite and made you miserable."

She wiped her eyes with her napkin. "You got that right, kiddo! I'm swearing off men forever!"

I couldn't help but smile at that. Just how long would that resolution hold? One week? Two? "You don't have to go to that extreme. Just try to see if you can't make yourself happy by finding a hobby or an interest that you can immerse yourself in."

"With the hours I work, that seems damned near impossible," she countered.

"Well, I admit that's a drawback. But maybe one evening a week, you could manage to join a group of some kind: play bridge or take dancing lessons or go to Sportime and work out."

"Who me? Work out?" She said it with a grin so I knew the old Meredith was back. "Besides, speak for yourself, Liz. What are you doing to get out and about?"

"Well, actually," I said, "I'm taking art classes."

"Good for you," she said, but immediately switched the conversation to her wardrobe. "Hey, you want to run over to Macy's? I need some new shoes."

"Thanks, but no." I wasn't that interested in shopping any more. I had next to zero social life, and all I needed to paint in

45

were jeans and T-shirts. My good outfits hung unused in my closet.

A few days later I was working in my studio when a knock came at the door.

"Come in," I called. I had a brush loaded with paint and didn't want to put it down.

The door opened and Rachel stepped in. "Oh, Liz, that's great," she exclaimed. Using a sketch I had made in my class, I was working on an acrylic painting of a nude. I knew it wasn't great, but I was pleased with my progress.

"Thanks, Rachel. I'm learning a lot from my class."

"Well, I have some good news too." She beamed.

I balanced my brush on the edge of my palette and gave her my full attention. Rachel had been so discouraged lately that I'd been afraid she was going to give up on her dream entirely. I hoped and prayed the good news had something to do with her writing. "Tell me quick. I can't stand the suspense."

"I've had a story accepted by one of the more prestigious literary magazines. I'm ecstatic!"

I grabbed her and gave her a hug. "I knew it was going to happen. Now you're on your way, babe."

"I don't know about that," she said. "But I was so close to quitting, and this has given me the impetus to keep on."

"We need to celebrate."

"I've already decided to have a party. I don't have the space at my condo, but I have permission to use the living room here. I'm inviting everyone who has a studio here and their significant others and some of my friends. I know a couple of guys who will provide some music. It won't be fancy. Some wine and cheese and crackers and good conversation. Why don't you invite someone to come with you?"

I perched on the edge of the desk. "I don't have anyone to

invite." I hated the idea of being the only one there without a companion. I was still having trouble getting used to that.

"You mentioned your art teacher the other day. From the way you talked, I thought you found him pretty interesting. Why not ask him?"

"He's probably already taken." I wouldn't admit to her that I had been thinking about him quite a bit and wondered if he was married or in a relationship.

"Does he wear a wedding ring?"

"No. But that doesn't mean he's unattached."

"How will you ever know unless you ask?"

"Oh, Rachel, I haven't done anything like that since college. I don't know a thing about the dating scene any more." The mere idea of dating gave me indigestion.

"Well, it's changed, that's for sure what with on-line match ups. But you can do it the good old fashioned way and ask somebody you know. After all, you're only asking him to go to a party with you. It's not like you're making a commitment." She had a grin on her face that said *I dare you to do it!*

"I don't know. . . ."

"Think about it," Rachel said. "Don't be a wuss."

"What if he is married?"

"Then I guess he'll say so and turn you down."

"I'll be so embarrassed."

"Don't be silly. There's nothing to be embarrassed about. He'll be flattered."


My next class was a couple of nights later. I still hadn't made up my mind whether or not I would ask Jay to the party. I didn't know how to approach him about it without feeling like an idiot.

That evening he'd recruited a street person to pose for us, fully clothed. He was an older man with stringy hair and a straggly beard and a face that showed a lot of hard living. But such an interesting face! I chose to draw his head and shoulders only with charcoal, trying to use what I'd learned about shadows and highlights which were displayed so prominently on his rugged face.

Jay looked at my work-in-progress. "You need to use more shadow here," he said, pointing to the side of the cheek. "Make it really dark. Then you can pull out the reflected light with your eraser. This gives the head more dimension."

I did as he suggested and was amazed at the difference it made.

When the class was over, I lingered over my sketch pad waiting for the rest of the class to leave. A couple of them dawdled, and I almost gave up and left. But I willed myself to stay put.

Finally only Jay and I were still in the room.

"Are you having some difficulty?" he asked as he walked over to me.

"Oh, no. Just finishing up," I said. My stomach was clenched in a spasm and my hands shook noticeably. It was now or never.

He was standing beside me now. I didn't dare look up at him but busied myself putting away my supplies. "Umm, Jay," I mumbled, "there's going to be a party celebrating a writer friend of mine who's had a story accepted for publication. I wondered if you'd be interested in going."

"Well, sure. Always want to support a fellow artist," he said enthusiastically. "When and where is it?"

"A week from Sunday at five at the Sternberger Artists' Center."

"I'll be there."

He hadn't asked where I lived, so apparently it hadn't occurred to him that I was asking him out. I realized he might even bring his own date. I couldn't very well explain now that I was asking him to go with me. My worst fears had been realized. I no longer knew how to take even baby steps to get back into the dating game.

For the next week I silently berated myself for botching such a simple thing as inviting a man to go out with me. I almost decided not to go to the party for fear of confronting Jay's significant other, but I realized what a selfish notion that was. The party was to celebrate Rachel's success, and I was ashamed of myself for being so focused on me.

Rachel and I had lunch together the following Tuesday. "Well, I've been waiting since last Friday to hear whether or not you invited your teacher to the party. Did you chicken out, Liz?"

I pretended to be studying the menu while I decided what to tell her. Finally I put it down. "I messed up."

"What do you mean?"

"I asked him, and he said yes. But I guess it came out wrong. He didn't seem to realize I was asking him to go with me. I expect him to show up with someone else."

Rachel grimaced. "Oh, my. That's too bad. However, it will answer the question for you whether he's in a relationship."

"Good point." Somehow I felt better after that.

Samantha had lingered in my thoughts all this time. When I finally got up enough nerve to see her again, I went to the motel office and asked what room she was in. With winter not all that far away, I thought she might need some warm clothes. I felt it was the least I could do for her. But the clerk at the motel told me she was no longer there, and I wondered if she'd returned to Wilmington. I couldn't help but feel some relief at that possibility. If she were no longer around, I could quit obsessing about her.

# CHAPTER SEVEN

The Sunday of Rachel's party I couldn't decide what to wear. I knew it was to be a casual occasion but I still fretted over what would look best. I hadn't dressed up at all for such a long time that I had trouble making a choice. Finally I settled on black slacks and sandals and a white blouse with a turquoise quilted jacket that I knew brought out the blue of my eyes. I took a curling iron to my short auburn hair which I usually just shampooed and combed. I kept telling myself Jay would probably have a woman with him, but I still changed my outfit three times.

It was a quarter after five when I arrived at the party, and it was already in full swing. I was introduced to husbands, wives, and others who I knew ranged from lovers to simply friends of the various Sternberger tenants. The large table normally in the middle of the living room had been pushed against the front wall and held bottles of wine in coolers along with trays holding crudités, dips, and cheese and crackers. In the little sunroom two guys with guitars were strumming away. Thankfully they were acoustic so it was possible to carry on a conversation over the music.

Jay wasn't there. I didn't know whether to be glad or disappointed. I'd been steeling myself for the probability he'd come with a woman, so that meant there was still hope. I circulated among the crowd, greeting the partygoers. Everyone who had a studio was there: Jeannette Mabry who had two novels published, one of which had even briefly made the New York Times bestseller list; Bonnie Wainright, a poet who had won numerous awards and had four books of poetry in print; Earl Bernard, a painter whose favorite subject was black musicians; Sean Northrup, who made fused glass jewelry, and Anthony Grunwald who wrote true crime books.

Every one of them had a significant other with them, and I'd never felt like such an odd man out. This was the first party I'd been to as a single woman and, frankly, I didn't feel comfortable. My pragmatic self realized I should quit being so concerned about my plight—if I could honestly call it that—and get into the celebratory mood of the occasion. This was Rachel's big day, and that needed to be my focus.

Rachel had a "date" that she introduced as Evan Stuart. Since she'd never mentioned to me that she had been going out with anyone, I was taken by surprise. Evan was noticeably younger than Rachel and extremely handsome which made me feel even more like a loser. They seemed so relaxed and at ease with each other, I had to assume that she'd known him for some time. Was this occasion in part to introduce Evan as the new man in her life?

I was sitting on the sofa in the foyer, taking a break from trying to make small talk with people I didn't know when the front door opened and Jay appeared—alone. It was a quarter to six and I'd given up any hope that he would show up.

"Liz," he said, panting as though trying to catch his breath. "I hope I haven't missed the festivities. I neglected to tell you I had business to attend to earlier in the afternoon, and I wasn't sure when I would be free. It went on longer than I expected."

He stood in the middle of the foyer and looked into the living room which still teemed with partygoers. "Well, it looks like it's still going strong."

I jumped up. Flustered by the emotions that had overtaken

me, I almost stuttered. I was so happy to see him, especially since he was alone, but I was sure he thought I'd been sitting there waiting for him. How embarrassing.

I willed myself to be calm and not seem too eager. "Glad you could make it, Jay. I was just taking a little break from all the noise and confusion." *I wasn't desperately waiting for you.* "Come on in and let me introduce you around."

Jay already knew some of the party goers. He and Earl Bernard apparently had known each other from way back.

"Earl, good to see you," Jay said, when we approached him. Earl looks like a pro tackle with broad shoulders and beefy arms. His bald head shone like a polished chestnut in the light from the wall sconces. He definitely is not the image of the effete artist. "I saw your newest work at the Green Hill Gallery. Good work!" Green Hill displays the work of top North Carolina artists, so I knew it had to be a prestigious show.

Earl threw his arm around Jay's shoulder. "This is my buddy, here," he said to me. "I took lessons from this guy when I was on the verge of dropping out of Dudley High. He helped me turn my life around." He punched Jay affectionately on the shoulder. "This dude has helped many sorry-ass kids get themselves straightened out."

"Naw, Earl, you straightened yourself out. I just showed you how much talent you had, and that was all you needed to know."

Earl grinned. "He can deny all he wants. But Jay's like a football coach to kids who have artistic talent. He pushes them hard. Even those who have minimal ability. He's a substitute dad for kids who don't have one."

I had no idea that Jay had served as a mentor to children. I'd admired his teaching skills, but this was a complete surprise.

"Earl here even got himself a minister's license," Jay said, looking like a proud father.

"Well, I got no church," Earl laughed, "but I do a bit of

preachin' here and there. I preach to kids to follow their dreams, just like Jay does."

Anthony Grunwald greeted Jay as an old friend as well.

"Melanie's enjoying your class a lot," he said.

"That's his fourteen-year-old daughter," Jay explained to me. "She's in my Saturday morning group."

"That's the only thing that could get her out of bed on a Saturday morning," Anthony said. "We'd enrolled her in all kinds of things like soccer and tennis. But she was never interested in them. Now she can hardly wait to go to class."

"Well, the girl *is* good. From what I can tell, no one at school had ever encouraged her before. That's all it takes."

"You underestimate your ability to connect to kids," Anthony said. "You have a special talent, Jay."

Jay seemed embarrassed and anxious to change the subject. "Where's the honoree?" he asked me. "I need to give her my congratulations."

Rachel was at the other end of the room talking to Bonnie Wainright. I guided Jay over to them after insisting he get a glass of wine and some cheese and crackers. I'd already had one glass of wine, usually my limit, but decided it would be more sociable to have another one with him. I'd sip it slowly and leave most of it in the goblet.

I introduced him to the two women.

He took Rachel's hand between his two slender hands that had always looked to me like a musician's with his long, tapered fingers. "I understand you are about to become a published author. And in a prestigious magazine! That is quite an accomplishment."

Rachel smiled broadly. "Thank you so much." She caught my eye for a second as if to say, S*ee, I knew he would show up—alone.*

Jay then turned to Bonnie. "I so admire your poetry, Bonnie.

Greensboro is fortunate to have such a wonderful talent."

"And I admire your paintings, Jay. I'm saving up to buy one."

I was feeling way out of their league. How did I think I could ever hold my own with all these talented people?

I was wondering why I thought I should have invited Jay when he took my arm and said, "Why don't you show me your studio?"

I felt hesitant. I had hung a number of my paintings and drawings on the walls using painters' tape, and I wasn't sure I wanted him to see my work. It seemed so second rate compared to what others in my class had been doing. I painted solely for my own pleasure, the process being therapeutic and healing which was what I cared about. The resulting picture was secondary; I never planned to show them to anyone. Of course Jay had seen the work I had done in class, but those were mostly studies, not finished pictures.

"It's pretty messy," I demurred.

"Of course it's messy. Painters can't afford to be anal about their surroundings. That would interfere with the process."

Much as I tried, I couldn't think of another excuse. "Well, it is a wonderful room," I said. "It was the library of the house, and next to the living room, I think I have the best room here. So please admire the architectural details. Forget I have paintings stuck on the walls."

Jay smiled at me. "We'll see."

I took him through the foyer and into the back hall to the door to my room. It also had a door into the living room, but I didn't want to enter that way where everyone could look in. No one else was in the back hall.

I unlocked the door and ushered him inside. The sun was close to setting, so I turned on the overhead light which gave off a harsh glare, unlike the soft daylight that flooded the room when I worked there.

He looked around. "I see what you mean. This is really nice, especially all the bookcases you have. Great place to keep art books and your materials. I imagine you get good light in here during the day."

"I do," I said. "I usually work from about nine until three or four, if I don't have other obligations."

He went over to study the pictures I'd stuck on the far wall. "Nice," he said. "I can see a definite progression here. You haven't been painting for very long, have you?"

We'd never discussed anything personal in class. "I've dabbled all my life," I said, "but I never had time to do anything serious with it. My husband died early this year and I decided that life is too short, and we should take the time to do the things we've always just talked about."

He turned around and faced me, his expression sympathetic. "I didn't realize that, Liz. I'm so sorry." He lowered his gaze before continuing, and his voice softened. "I happen to know how you feel. My wife of twenty-six years died last year."

I was shocked; I never had a clue he was a widower. "Please accept my condolences then," I said.

"If you're like I am, you'll find solace in the act of painting."

"That's what it's all about for me. I don't expect to become very good at it. I just know that it's making me whole again."

"Don't denigrate your ability," he said gruffly. "You have a great deal of talent, Liz. I can see a marked improvement already in the short time you've been in my class. You'll be participating in shows one of these days."

I could see the man Earl Bernard had described, the one who gave pep talks to the kids who had little faith in themselves. I was sure he was using his coaching skills on me and took it with a grain of salt. But it did feel good.

We returned to the living room, and Jay stayed till almost the last guest had left. He offered his help to Rachel to clean up afterward, but she declined saying she and Evan could handle it.

"Do you have a way home, Liz?" he asked me.

"I live a couple of blocks from here," I said. "I walked over."

"Then let me walk you home. It's getting dark."

I didn't argue with him. Summit Avenue isn't the safest place after dark. I hadn't intended to stay so long and thought I could get home before the sun went down. So it was a relief to have an escort.

We chatted about the party and class, and we were at my front door in no time.

"What a charming house," he said. "I live in an older house in Summerfield, but I've been too busy to do much fixing up. Did you and your husband do all this restoration?"

"It took us years doing a little at a time, but we loved it."

"I can see why."

"So how are you getting home, Jay?"

"My car is over behind Sternberger. I could have driven you home, but it seemed like a lovely night for a short stroll."

We shook hands and said we'd see each other again on Thursday in class and he left.

I was so wound up I didn't get to sleep until after three.

# CHAPTER EIGHT

Rachel was in her studio when I arrived at the artists' center Monday morning. She hurried out to the back hall when she heard me unlock the back door.

"Great party, Rachel," I said as she greeted me all smiles.

"It was, wasn't it? And I liked your teacher a lot. He seemed to know several of the people who have studios here."

"Well, the art community is a pretty tightly knit group I now realize. But I hadn't known how much he had championed young artists. Earl gives him credit for encouraging him when he was a kid. Apparently he's helped a lot of kids stay out of trouble by giving them lessons."

"And I'm sure you were relieved that he showed up alone," Rachel said, grinning.

"He lost his wife recently. But that doesn't necessarily mean he's not interested in someone else. He was late because he came straight from a meeting."

Rachel's grin disappeared. "That's sad about his wife. But don't downgrade your chances with him. You never know what could develop."

"I'm not holding my breath. On the other hand, Rachel, have you been holding out on me? Who was that gorgeous fellow you were with?"

Her smile returned. "Evan? He's a neighbor of mine, an up-and-coming architect. He is gorgeous, isn't he? As it happens, his partner Will thinks so too. Will was out of town so he couldn't make the party. They are about the nicest neighbors I've ever had."

"Oh, shoot, I thought you two had something going."

"Well, it's my loss. Sometimes I think gays make the best friends of all. The ones I know are so kind and intuitive. It's to our detriment they don't want to hook up with girls."

"That's been my experience too."

We both went to our studios and worked for most of the day. I found I had an extra impetus to work as I wanted to please Jay at my next class.

On Thursday night Jay seemed distracted as he drifted around the class, making a suggestion here, a compliment there. He treated me the same as before last Sunday; I'd hoped that there would be at least an implicit acknowledgement of our time together by a word or gesture, but there was none of that. I'm sure I was expecting too much. But I have to admit I was sorely disappointed.

In Friday morning's paper I saw a short article on page ten: Brian Kadlacek, 16, arrested for selling marijuana. I'd checked the phone book when I first started my art classes, curious to learn where Jay lived. And he was the one and only Kadlacek in the directory. I realized Brian could be his son.

I felt awful for him. I didn't think I knew him well enough to broach the subject but wished there was some way I could offer help to ease a painful situation.

Finally I decided to ask Rachel what she would do. I wasn't trying to spread gossip—it was in the paper after all—and since she had once admitted to me that she'd smoked weed in college, I thought she could put it in perspective. Since I'd never had children, I had no idea how one would cope with such a matter.

"Yes, I noticed the article," Rachel said when I brought the subject up over lunch. "I wondered if he was related to Jay."

"I'm assuming so since there aren't any other Kadlaceks in the phone directory. Of course there could be unlisted numbers under that name."

"I know how to find out discreetly," she said. "I think Evan knows him. I'll ask him."

"Please don't tell him why you're asking."

She made a call from the phone in the front hall when we got back to the artists' center. I went into my studio because I didn't want to listen to the conversation. I felt a bit wretched as though I were intruding into Jay's private life. On the other hand, my curiosity was over the top.

A few minutes later Rachel came knocking on my door.

"Brian is Jay's son. He's an only child. Evan says Brian's been having kind of a rough time since his mother died."

"It must be really tough for a teenager to lose his mother. Poor kid. Poor Jay."

"Well, it is sad. But the fact he's a teenager is fortunate. Jay still has some control over what happens to him now. If he were in his twenties, his hands would be pretty much tied."

"Do you think I should say something to Jay? Or should I stay out of it?"

"If you approach it right, I think it would be a good idea. He's probably wishing his wife were here so they could discuss it. I think he might like a woman's point of view."

"I can't speak from experience since I don't have kids. He might think I'm just butting in."

"I think you found out Sunday how Jay steps in to help kids in trouble. I don't see why he'd object if you thought you could be of some help."

But can I be? Or am I just looking to make some Brownie points with him?

I debated with myself the whole week. I still hadn't decided what to do when I went to class on Thursday. Jay seemed as subdued as he had been the week before, and I had trouble concentrating on my drawing.

Once more I lingered when the class was over, waiting till all the other students had left. Jay was straightening up the room and didn't seem to notice me. Finally I went over to him while he was washing out brushes and cleared my throat.

He turned around from the sink, startled. "Liz! I didn't realize you were still here."

"I was wondering if you were up for a cup of coffee," I said.

I could see the indecision in his expression. Finally he said, "Sure. Just give me a minute till I get these brushes clean. They're so expensive I have to make sure I get all the paint out."

I sat on the edge of the platform where the models posed, waiting for him to finish. Finally he had everything put away.

"Where do you want to go?" he asked.

"How about the Green Bean?"

"One of my favorite places. Walk or ride?"

"It's nice out. Why don't we walk?"

We didn't talk as we strolled over to Elm Street and turned south toward the Green Bean, several blocks away. I guess each of us was waiting for the other to initiate the conversation.

Once we reached the coffee shop and had ordered our drinks, I thought it was up to me to say something. After all, I had invited him out.

"I wanted to thank you for coming to the party last week."

Jay looked up from stirring cream into his coffee. "It was nice. A lot of my favorite people were there."

I wished he meant me when he said that, but I'm sure he was talking about his artist friends.

"Well, Rachel appreciated your coming. This was a big deal for her. She's been trying to get something published for a very long time. I think she was on the verge of giving it all up. Getting that story published came in the nick of time."

"You always pray things will happen that way—arrive in the nick of time," he said with a hint of desperation. I guessed he was talking about intervention for Brian.

I felt tongue-tied at first. Then I decided just to go for it. "Jay, I saw the article in the paper."

He looked at me forlornly before he looked down at his coffee cup as if searching for an answer there. A worry line appeared in his forehead, and he was biting his lower lip. But he seemed incapable of saying anything.

Feeling awkward now, I said, "I was just wondering if there was anything I could do. I realize I have no experience with kids, but I think sometimes it just helps to talk it over with someone. I'm more than willing to be your listening post."

He was quiet for so long, I decided I'd really blown it. What a damn fool I was! I could feel a hot flush rising in my face.

I began studying my coffee too. We looked like two soothsayers trying to fathom our fortune in our drink. But I was simply trying to avoid his eyes. When I finally could stand it no longer, I looked up at him and saw he was staring at me.

"That's so kind of you, Liz," he said in a choked voice. "This has been such a blow. I've worked so hard trying to rescue kids from poverty and neglect that I guess I didn't give my own boy enough attention."

"I don't think you should beat yourself up. I'm sure it has much more to do with losing his mother than it does with you. The teenage years are the worst time possible for something like that to happen."

"He took it really hard. They were very close."

"Are the cops going to take that into consideration? Mitigating circumstances?"

"He's on probation and has to do community service. But I

think it has more to do with the fact that it's his first offence than it does with the loss of his mother."

"Well, I'm relieved to know that he's on probation. How long does that last?"

"Six months."

"That will go by fast."

Jay looked very solemn now. I thought he would be relieved that Brian hadn't been sent to juvenile detention. Finally he reached over and took my hand. "I was going to ask you out, Liz. I want to get to know you better. But for now I need to concentrate on my son. I'm afraid what his reaction would be if I start dating. Do you understand?"

My heart was doing flip flops. I didn't know what to say. I was so elated and so disappointed simultaneously. What else could I say to him except, "Yes, I understand, Jay." I even managed not to cry until we got back to the parking garage behind the Cultural Arts Center and I was safely in my car on the way home.

# CHAPTER NINE

The autumn days rolled slowly by. I painted at my studio during the day and went to class on Thursday nights. Jay was kind but maintained a somewhat distant attitude toward me. I didn't know whether he'd lost interest or deliberately held back so he wouldn't be distracted by thoughts of a possible involvement with me when things calmed down at home. At first I would day dream of having a relationship with him, wondering if it could ever happen, but I soon decided it was pointless to dwell on such an unlikelihood. I would only make myself miserable.

The holidays came and I wanted to pretend the season didn't exist. It would be the first Christmas without Peter, and I found that all the merriment around me only heightened my loneliness. I refused to put up a tree or decorate the house as it seemed so pointless to do it for myself. I couldn't stand to turn on the TV to be assaulted even by the carols in the commercials. I'd planned to spend the day reading and eating peanut butter sandwiches.

But Meredith insisted that I come to her condo for Christmas dinner. As far as I knew she never cooked, preferring to eat at the nice restaurants around town, but she told me she was fixing a turkey and couldn't possibly eat it all by herself. No amount of excuses could get me off the hook. I hadn't seen her in some time—she claimed that her workload was bigger than ever—and to be truthful I hadn't missed her very much. I found that her negative attitude tended to wear me down. I had enough negatives in my life already. But I finally gave in. I have a hard time discarding old friends, no matter how irritating they are.

She asked me to come around one P.M. "Let's have a midday meal. Then we can chill out the rest of the day."

I didn't want to spend the whole day with her, so I had an excuse ready so I could leave by mid-afternoon.

I'd been to her place a few times though we usually met at a centrally located restaurant since Grandover is a fairly long drive from my house and downtown. Her home is always gorgeous, but this time I marveled at the beautiful holiday decorations and huge live tree embellished within an inch of its life. Meredith had never before gotten into the Christmas spirit with much enthusiasm. I didn't know what had come over her.

When she moved into her condo, she had hired an interior designer who furnished it in a sophisticated style that featured soft natural shades ranging from doeskin to russet. It sounds bland, but she combined beautiful fabrics of different textures and patterns that contrasted with the Brazilian red oak floor. It is so stunning it was featured in a local magazine. Now greenery and dried flowers that blended with her color scheme adorned the mantel and tables and were even entwined in the living room chandelier. The ceiling-high tree glittered with hundreds of tiny lights and the limbs were filled with filmy bows and nosegays of dried baby's breath and white roses.

"My gosh, Meredith," I exclaimed as I entered her living room. "I didn't know you were so into Christmas. You never had a tree before, did you?"

"Isn't it beautiful?" She was obviously pleased as punch.

"It is. But why now?"

She led me over to the fawn suede sectional couch and sat down beside me. "I've decided I should stop trying to please men and concentrate on pleasing myself. I've wasted too much time worrying about my relationships with them. All it's done is made me crazy. I've got a good life without them, and I'm going to live it to the hilt."

I could hardly believe my ears. This wasn't the man-crazy Meredith that I'd known for so long. Was she finally growing up?

I hadn't intended to say anything to her about Jay, first, because I didn't know how she'd react, and second, because I figured she'd bring him up every time we were together. But her statement so caught me off guard, I found myself telling her all about him over the sumptuous dinner she'd prepared. I suppose I thought we could make some kind of a girlish pact that we would swear off men together. But that was for her benefit. In my secret heart of hearts I was still hoping that someday Jay would ask me out again.

"Oh, Liz," she gushed when I described him and told her about the party at the artists' center. "He sounds like a good catch. Are you going out with him now?"

I explained the situation with Brian. "He said he'd planned to ask me out, but when this happened, he felt that he needed to concentrate on his son for a while. It seems he took his mother's death very hard, and Jay was afraid he'd resent another woman in his father's life."

Meredith chewed on her food as she thought this over. Finally she said, "Well, I guess that's very noble of him, but I would stay away from him, Liz. He'll always put his son first and he'd break your heart."

"I don't know if that's necessarily true. This is a special situation. It isn't going to last forever."

"Mark my words. If you ever fell for him, it would be a disaster."

I didn't know whether to believe Meredith or not. True, she had many more experiences with men than I had. But she'd made such bad choices she'd become cynical. I would hate to paint every man in the universe with the same brush. All the same, it bothered me and put a pall on the rest of the day. Finally I dredged up my excuse that a friend from Sternberger was planning to come over in the late afternoon. Actually I had planned to invite Rachel to my house, even though she didn't observe Christmas, but she was one of many of the Jewish faith who served Christmas dinner to the homeless. I would have joined her but I'd already accepted Meredith's invitation.

That evening I lay in bed going over and over our conversation in my mind. I thought about Jay's recent remoteness. Was it because he was wrapped up in his son's problems, or had he simply lost all interest in me? Would I ever find out?

Painting had filled a void in my life and was giving me much pleasure. But it wasn't quite enough. And I knew I couldn't continue to dwell on whether or not Jay would ever be a part of my life. I had become too self-involved, and since I no longer delivered meals on wheels once a month, I wasn't doing any service to others. I felt a nagging sense of shame that I hadn't given back more to my community.

The week after Christmas when Rachel and I were having lunch together, she talked about serving the holiday dinner to the homeless at Weaver House on Lee Street.

"I've done it other years, but the need seems to be so much greater now, so I've decided to volunteer weekly. A lot of them are the chronic homeless, of course, people with mental illness or alcoholics. But now we see people who had homes but lost their jobs or were wiped out by medical bills. It breaks my heart."

"Do they need more volunteers?" I asked.

"Sure. Why don't you come with me? I go Wednesday mornings," Rachel said with an encouraging smile.

"I'd like to try it."

And so the following Wednesday I parked near Rachel's place on South Elm Street, and we walked the three blocks to Urban Ministry where Potter House is located. It was blustery cold with snowflakes swirling around us. I shivered in spite of my heavy winter coat and layers of silk underwear, T-shirt and sweater underneath. I couldn't conceive of being homeless on a day such as this.

We spent a couple of hours dishing up hearty breakfasts and serving it in a room filled with people of all ages, races, and circumstances. I was filled with a torrent of emotions: sorrow at the scope of the need in our town; revulsion, I'm ashamed to admit, at some of the dirty and bedraggled souls; pity for those who were obviously new to the state of homelessness; a sense of satisfaction at being able to do a little to help assuage their hunger. It was heartbreaking, and it was gratifying all at the same time.

We continued to serve weekly, and I was getting to know a lot of the regulars who came to Potter House. There were only single men and women there; families went to Pathways Family Center. It was hard enough to see adults who had no home. I couldn't imagine what it must be like for those with children.

One Wednesday in late January Rachel and I decided to drive to Potter House instead of walk. It was the coldest, most miserable day of the year and the wind whipped around buildings like a howling banshee. I was afraid I wasn't going to make it from the car to the building without turning into a pillar of ice.

The dining room was fuller than ever. I figured that people who had so far resisted coming to a shelter had surrendered to the inevitable: get inside or face the prospect of hypothermia. There were a number of new faces that I didn't recognize.

I'd been serving for a half hour or so when I looked across the room and saw a familiar face. She wore a navy blue watch cap over straggly hair but it didn't hide the strangely tilted ears. The down-sloped eyes and flattened nose were unmistakable.

I set down the plate I'd been carrying in front of a regular, an older woman whose face bore all the ravages of time and hard living, and hurried over to the other side of the room.

"Samantha?"

She looked up at me without recognition.

"I'm Mrs. Raynor. Remember, you came to my house last summer looking for my husband?"

She blinked a couple of times. "I guess."

"What are you doing here, Samantha? I thought you were living in a motel."

She looked down at the table and said in a quiet voice, "I ran out of money."

"Where are you staying?"

"Here."

I knew that people could stay there only ninety days, and then they had to leave. "When did you come here?"

"A few weeks ago."

I didn't know why I hadn't seen her before. Maybe she'd skipped breakfast those days. Maybe she had been ill.

"Can I do anything for you, Samantha?"

She shook her head no, refusing to look at me. I stood beside her for a few minutes but it was evident she had nothing more to say so I left.

I spent the rest of the morning serving meals in a fog. I couldn't get Samantha out of my mind. The homeless had taken on a familiar face, and I found it quite disturbing. It's a little easier to hold yourself aloof from the problems of others when it doesn't touch your life in a personal way. Samantha, whom I barely knew, had nevertheless made it personal.

# CHAPTER TEN

Rachel and I had lunch together the next day. I'd lain awake for hours the night before wondering what circumstances had brought Samantha to Greensboro and what kind of a future she might have.

I told Rachel that I had encountered someone I knew while serving breakfast the day before. I would have preferred to dismiss Samantha from my thoughts, but I couldn't seem to do that. I thought talking it over could help.

"Seriously?" she said her voice full of concern. "Is it someone you know well? Do you know what happened to her? Or is it a he? Gosh, that's sad."

"I really know next to nothing about her," I said. "And yes, it is a she. Which worries me more than if it were a man. I figure it's easier for men to get back on their feet."

"Some of our clients might argue that point with you. But, yes, if a man is drug- and alcohol-free and in good health, he can probably get a job sooner or later. Women aren't always that lucky."

"And this woman . . . well, I'm not real sure about her. She could be borderline developmentally disabled. But she might not be. She has an unusual appearance which makes me wonder." I shook my head. "It's hard to tell."

Rachel gave me a sad smile. "How do you know her, Liz?"

"Last summer she came to my door looking for Peter. She got very upset when I told her he had died. But I couldn't get anything out of her about how she knew him. It was very strange." *And I've been in denial ever since about what that connection might be.*

"Is she from around here?"

"No, she said she was from Wilmington. But she had a beat up old suitcase with her. It was obvious she didn't plan to go back there."

"So what were her plans?"

"She asked me about motels, so I took her to the one up on Summit which I knew had weekly rates, and I thought it would be fairly safe there."

Rachel sipped her iced tea thoughtfully. "Did she tell you why she was at the shelter now?"

"She ran out of money, pure and simple."

Neither of us said anything for a few minutes. I knew Rachel was trying to digest this information and decide what she could ask without upsetting me, the kinds of questions that I'd been mentally warding off because I didn't want to deal with them.

Finally she spoke. "Do you have any clue as to how she might have known Peter?" She was looking at me with sympathy and almost seemed reluctant to ask the question. But she probably thought it would be more telling if she didn't. Unspoken thoughts can loom large.

This, of course, was the crux of the matter. *How did she know Peter?*

I'd tell her what I'd been telling myself all these months. "I had two thoughts. Peter used to help out with the Special Olympics. I wondered if he'd met her there."

"You said you weren't sure whether she was developmentally disabled or not."

*Oh, Rachel, let's not go there. I really don't want to explore this.*
"That's true. I was basing that on her appearance, and I shouldn't have."

"Can you describe her? I probably saw her too."

I told her about the strangely placed ears, the sloped eyes and thick neck, and the posture similar to some older people with osteoporosis. I tried to describe the clothes she had been wearing when I saw her at the shelter.

"Oh, yeah, I remember seeing her. I didn't get a chance to talk to her though."

"She seems very shy. Doesn't have much to say."

"But, if she came from Wilmington, that makes it very hard to figure out how she knew Peter, doesn't it?" Rachel asked.

"Peter had some clients there. They started with him years ago when they lived in Greensboro and wanted to stay with him even after they moved. So he still handled their accounts. You know I told you we used to go to Holden Beach pretty often? He always scheduled a run up to Wilmington to visit several sets of clients there."

"Did you ever go with him and meet them?"

"Are you kidding? And miss a day on the beach? We only had one car down there, and I couldn't have gone off sightseeing in Wilmington while he was working. I just stayed at the cottage."

"So she might have been a client?"

"More like the daughter of one, I think."

Rachel sipped her tea. "Yeah, I guess if she's run out of money, her parents might have lost their investments. Do you think they're aware she's homeless? Surely they wouldn't let that happen if they knew."

"Well, that thought did occur to me in this downturn. A lot of stock portfolios have tanked. I wondered if that happened to her family."

Rachel could see where I was going with this. She reached across the table and patted my hand. "Whatever happened, Liz, *it is not your fault!* Remember that."

"I'm trying, I'm trying," I said.

Even though I'd told Rachel I was trying not to feel any responsibility for Samantha's plight, I couldn't bear the thought of her being put out on the street at the end of her ninety days at the shelter. The job market was as bad as it ever had been in town so I didn't think I'd be able to help find her a job so she could support herself. And I wasn't at all sure what she was capable of doing anyway.

I decided the following Wednesday I'd invite Samantha to have dinner with me that evening. Maybe then I could get some answers. I wanted to help the young woman get back on her feet.

She didn't show up until my shift was nearly over. I was wondering if she'd found a place to live; surely, I hoped, she wasn't back on the streets, not in this weather. It wasn't quite as cold as it had been the previous week, but it was still in the thirties.

She trailed in toward the end of the breakfast seating. I heaped up a plate with food and carried it over to her. Since she was late, there was an empty seat beside her so I sat down.

"Hello, Samantha," I said, "how are you today?"

She looked a little startled. "Okay, I guess." Her voice was soft, barely audible. And she sounded depressed. But how could she *not be* under the circumstances?

"I was wondering if you would like to have dinner at my house this evening."

She had begun eating and didn't answer for a minute. "They feed me here," she said finally.

"I know that. I just wanted to have a chance to get to know you better."

She ate some more. Then she looked at me and asked, "Why?"

Apparently Samantha didn't believe in the usual niceties of

polite conversation. She got to the point immediately without pretension. In a way it reminded me of Meredith only in a much more innocent way.

"Well, I just would," I said, not afraid of being disingenuous myself. I thought if I told her I wanted to find out how she knew Peter, she would never come.

"Okay," she said and turned back to her breakfast.

I got up from the table. "I'll pick you up at six o'clock. Please wait by the front door and I'll honk when I get here. I drive a white car."

She said nothing more, so I went back to the serving table. Rachel, who'd been at the far end of the serving line, came over and began dishing up food next to me.

"I saw you talking to Samantha. Did you learn anything?"

"I invited her to dinner tonight. Thought maybe I'd find out something then."

"Good idea." She plopped a mound of fried potatoes on a plate.

"I don't know. It's like pulling teeth to get anything out of her. She might not tell me anything." I was dishing up sausages and the smell was making me hungry.

"Well, if you can establish a relationship with her, she might finally open up."

"Maybe," I said. "Then, again, maybe not."

I decided to fix meatloaf, baked potatoes, green beans and a salad. That was typical of the unimaginative meals I put together when I did any cooking at all. After my brief fling with trying new recipes while I was painting still lifes, I'd lost interest again. Looking back, I realize she might have enjoyed something special that she didn't ordinarily get. I could have gotten carry out from one of the good restaurants, but it didn't occur to me at the time.

I became increasingly nervous as the day went by. What was I going to ask her? I knew I had to lead up to my real question gradually without putting her off. She was so hard to talk to I was afraid I'd end up talking to myself. I began to wonder if this had been a good idea.

I arrived at the shelter five minutes early. I didn't see Samantha inside the glass door and wondered if I'd have to go inside and track her down. But a minute before six she appeared. She was dressed in jeans, as always, and an oversized dark blue anorak that hung down over her gloveless hands showing only her fingertips. She had on the watch cap I'd seen earlier pulled down over her ears and forehead. I honked and she came slowly out the door and over to the car.

"Hello, Samantha," I said as she settled in the passenger seat.

"Hi," she said, without a smile as she fastened the seat belt.

Neither of us spoke during the ten minutes it took to drive to my house.

Once inside, I took her coat and hat and stashed them in the coat closet, then led her to the dining room. "I have dinner ready," I told her. "Have a seat here, and I'll bring it in." I had set the table with my good china and water goblets. I'd even bought a small bouquet of flowers from Harris Teeter for a centerpiece. I might be serving plain food, but I wanted a festive atmosphere.

I'd already made up the salad plates and brought them to the table. Then I filled two plates with food and served them. "Water or tea?" I asked.

"Water," she said, so I brought in two glasses of water and settled into my seat across the table from her.

"Shall we have grace?" I asked.

She nodded and proceeded to recite it to my surprise. "Dear Lord, bless this food to the nourishment of our bodies and us to Thy service. In Christ's name we pray. Amen."

Those were the most words I had heard her say.

I could hear the ticking of the grandfather clock and the ping of forks on the china while we ate as I deliberately waited a few minutes before questioning her. I didn't want her to think I'd invited her to my house to grill her even though it was pretty evident. When the silence became unbearable I spoke. "How is it living at the shelter?" I asked.

"It's okay. Better than being on the streets."

"Were you ever staying on the streets?"

"For a couple of weeks. When they kicked me out of the motel because I couldn't pay, I didn't know where to go. I sat in the downtown library during the day and slept in an abandoned house someone told me about at night. But I was scared. And cold. Then I went to the shelter."

I was horrified for the girl, but I tried not to show it. I couldn't imagine what it would be like not to have a roof over your head.

"Are you trying to find a job?" I hoped she wouldn't resent me for asking that. She probably thought I had a lot of nerve to ask personal questions.

She looked me steadily in the eye. "Would you hire me?"

She took me by surprise, leaving me speechless. Finally I stuttered. "I . . . I . . . don't have a business. I'm retired."

"That's not what I meant. Would you hire me if you *were* a businesswoman, the way I look?"

What a question. Her bluntness was a challenge I wasn't accustomed to, unless you counted Meredith, whom I usually ignored. I hesitated a moment and I knew that gave me away. "Of course I would, Samantha. I judge people on their personal qualities." *Not their appearance* I added to myself. But I wasn't sure that was true.

She rolled her eyes, nodded, and went back to eating. I felt like a fool.

I was sick at heart and wondered if the whole evening had been wrecked because of my blatantly insincere response.

"I want to help you find a job if you'd like me to. I don't have anything specific in mind, but I could ask around." I hoped that would compensate for my pathetic answer and give me a chance to find out more about her. "Can you tell me what your skills are? Can you use a computer?"

"I can hunt and peck. But I don't know any of the fancy programs you need to know for a job."

"What's your schooling? Have you worked before?"

"I have a GED. I've worked at fast food restaurants, but I'd like to do something better."

With only a GED, I doubted that would be possible. "Have you thought of going to community college? Get a specific skill that would get you a job?"

"I dropped out of school because I was the butt of so many jokes. I couldn't deal with it." She hugged herself as she worked to control her emotions. "I don't think I could face going to class again."

I knew how cruel kids can be, especially if your appearance differs from the norm. I had a lazy eye when I was a child. I hated the way I looked and wished I could have worn sunglasses 24/7 to hide it. I was an adult before I had an operation to straighten it. And my "defect" was minimal compared to what Samantha had to deal with.

"You know, Samantha," I said, "by the time you go to community college, the students are mature. You'd find all kinds of people there and all ages. It's a whole different place."

She shrugged. "Doesn't make much difference. I don't have any money."

"I could look into that. I bet I could find some kind of scholarship for you."

She stared at me. "You'd do that?" Her expression said she

76

wasn't convinced. Probably too many promises had been made to her that never materialized.

"Of course I would." Was I promising more than I could possibly pull off?

She smiled for a moment, but the joy quickly left her face and the sadness returned. "I can't go to school if I don't have a place to live."

"I could look into that, too."

She stared at me for a couple of minutes. "Why are you doing this? You don't know me."

This seemed to be the perfect opening for the question I longed to ask. "No, but apparently you knew my husband."

She shook her head. "Not really."

"But you came looking for him. How did you know Peter?"

She settled back in her chair. "I heard my mom say his name."

"Was she one of his customers? What's her name?"

"Ella Graves. She died last year. What do you mean customer?"

"My husband was a financial advisor. He had some clients in Wilmington." Though Peter sometimes talked about his customers, I didn't recall ever hearing the name Ella Graves.

"I guess she must have been. All I know is that before she died she said if I had a problem about money, to look up Peter Raynor in Greensboro."

"Oh, my gosh, Samantha. I wish you'd told me sooner. All his files were turned over to another man. I can check it out for you."

Her face lit up again. "Would you do that?" She seemed unable to believe that I would do anything on her behalf.

"Of course. What about your father?"

"He died several years ago. I don't have any other relatives."

So Samantha was all alone in the world. She was one of those individuals who apparently had the cards stacked against her.

My life seemed so ordered compared to hers. How could I feel sorry for myself anymore?

# CHAPTER ELEVEN

I made promises that night that I wasn't at all sure I could keep.

I needed to see if there was any money in investments that her mother might have left her, if indeed Peter had managed her portfolio. It seemed to me that would have been handled when her mother died, but I could check it out anyway.

I called Ron Pemberton who had taken over Peter's clients when he became ill. I hadn't talked to him since the funeral. Though he had also taken over my own investments, I guess he thought the monthly statements were sufficient. It had rankled me quite a bit that he had taken my account for granted and assumed I didn't need any hand holding. I'd thought occasionally about changing financial advisors though I'd never gotten around to doing anything about it yet.

"Liz!" he exclaimed. "Good to hear from you. How are you?"

A little late to be asking me that, isn't it? "I'm doing well, thank you."

"I . . . uh . . . I've been so crazy busy with the economy unraveling that I haven't had time to call you. Sorry about that."

*Sure, sure. That's as good an excuse as any.* "No problem, Ron. I just hoped you could help me with something."

"Absolutely! Of course!" The guilt in his voice was almost comical. Almost.

"I wanted to ask about a former client of Peter's. I've met her daughter recently, and she doesn't seem to know anything about her mother's investments."

"Can't she ask her mother?"

"She died last year."

"Sorry," he said, "I can't help you. I only have files on current clients so I wouldn't have any information on her." So much for that idea. Whatever money Ella Graves might have had, her daughter was now penniless.

First things first I thought. If I could find some kind of a job for her, then she could afford to rent a room at least. But with only a GED that wasn't going to be easy. I wished I had more contacts around town, favors that I could call in.

If anyone could call in favors, it would be Meredith. She knew most of the movers and shakers in town. I called her and made an appointment to meet her for lunch the next day.

We met downtown at the 223 South Elm restaurant because she said she didn't have a lot of time. "Other businesses may be hurting, but we aren't," she said. "We have more patent applications than ever." I could only hope that was a sign that the economy would eventually turn around.

We both ordered southern herb fried green tomato BLTs.

It had been weeks since we'd been together so we chatted for a while about our personal lives.

"It sounds like we're both leading celibate lives," she said when I told her I only saw Jay at my Thursday night art classes. "Who'd have thought? Not that I'm thinking this is a permanent situation for me. Just for now. How about you, Liz?"

"I've decided to take it a day at a time. If Jay doesn't ever express interest in me again, maybe someone else will show up. Or not. I'm not obsessing over it."

"Obsession. That's a good word. I used to obsess whether or not there was a man in my life. Not any more though. I keep busy enough I don't even miss them."

We ate for a little while in silence. Finally I brought up the subject of Samantha.

"Remember I told you about the woman who showed up at my door last fall asking for Peter?"

"Yeah. What about her?"

"I've begun volunteering at Urban Ministry once a week serving breakfast. And she's staying there."

"In the homeless shelter?"

"Yes. She ran out of money and got kicked out of the motel I took her to."

"That's a shame."

At one time Meredith believed that homeless people brought it on themselves through laziness or by being alcoholics or addicted to drugs. She didn't have a lot of sympathy for them. But since even middle-class people had been so adversely affected by the economy, she'd become more compassionate towards the subject. I knew she'd begun donating to organizations like Urban Ministry.

"I'm really worried about her, Meredith. They can only stay there for ninety days and then they're out on the street again."

"But what can you do about it, Liz? And why are you so concerned about her? You have no obligation to her." She pulled out her compact and checked her makeup as if dismissing the subject of Samantha.

But I wasn't going to drop the subject. True, I wasn't obliged to help the young woman. But the fact she'd come to my home looking for Peter haunted me. It was a very tenuous connection, but I couldn't seem to shrug it off. "I don't know, I just feel compelled to help her. I want to get her out of there and at least into a room at a boarding house."

Meredith fluffed her hair, still looking at the mirror. "Does she have any skills?"

"That's the problem. She has a GED, but only basic

computer skills. If she could earn a little money somewhere, I hoped she could get a scholarship to the community college. Learn a trade of some sort."

She closed the compact with a snap. "That's a big order. It's hard for people with tons of experience to get a job nowadays. I don't think she's got much of a chance."

"The one thing in her favor is that she'd be cheap labor. You have all kinds of connections, Meredith. Couldn't you put in a good word for her somewhere?"

"Has she applied at fast food restaurants?" She was studying her check now, obviously weary of the conversation.

"That was the one thing she hoped she wouldn't have to do. Apparently she once worked at one. I don't think it was a good experience."

"Beggars can't be choosers."

That was an unfortunate choice of words I thought. Samantha had been reduced to the role of a beggar. "I was thinking something like a filing job, a gofer for someone."

"Let me think on it and see what I can do. I'll get back to you. But I've got to run." She put money in the folder with the bill and scooted out of her seat. " 'Bye, Liz," she said as she hurried toward the door. I wondered if she'd even remember what she'd promised.

My art class was that evening. If it hadn't been for my overwhelming desire to improve my painting skills, I would have considered quitting it. Being around Jay was like being on a strict diet and having double fudge chocolate cake waved beneath my nose. It drove me crazy. He was friendly enough and helpful when it came to questions about painting, but he treated me no differently than any other student in the class. I know it was childish to hold onto an infatuation, and I was sure that's all it was, when the focus of that desire has no interest in you.

When the class was over and I was putting away my paints and brushes, Jay walked by and whispered, "Stick around for a bit, will you?" I'm embarrassed to relate how thrilled I was by that innocuous request. And then it occurred to me he probably wanted to talk about class work.

When all the other students had left, he came back to where I was puttering around trying to look busy. "Cup of coffee?"

We drove our separate cars to a fast food restaurant on Market Street where we got our coffees and settled into a booth. At this time in the evening there were few other customers, which gave our meeting an intimate feel.

I concentrated on stirring the cream into my cup waiting for Jay to start the conversation.

"It's been really hard for me these past months," he began. "I had to think of you as just another student. If I dwelt on how much I wanted to get to know you better, I couldn't have concentrated on doing what was right for my son."

He paused, waiting for my response.

I decided I might as well be truthful. "I thought you'd lost interest. You seemed really distant."

He looked stricken. "That was self-preservation, Liz. I couldn't handle it any other way. I'm sorry if I hurt you."

I shrugged. No use in telling him how much I thought about him. I'd come off sounding like a lovelorn teenager.

He gripped his paper cup with both hands and looked at me steadily. "What I wanted to tell you was that I seem to have the situation with my son under control. I was hoping you'd be willing to go out with me now. That is, if you aren't totally put off by my behavior." He gave me a weak, hopeful smile.

I felt like jumping up and down and shouting, yes, yes! My memories of Peter were precious and would always be with me, but I needed to make a new life. I contained myself and nodded. "I'm willing to give it a try," I said, trying not to sound overanxious.

We decided to go to dinner and a movie on Saturday night. He asked me to choose the restaurant, and since I thought he probably didn't have a lot of money, I suggested Irving Park Delicatessen. "I haven't been there in ages," I said, "and it's close to the Carousel Theater."

"Good choice. Pick you up at six?"

I sang along with Carrie Underwood on the car radio all the way home, even though I can't carry a tune.

The next morning at Sternberger I caught Rachel on her way into her studio.

"The wait is over," I told her.

She looked at me strangely for a moment before realization dawned and she broke into a huge smile. "Jay!" was all she said.

I nodded. I'd told her what had happened after her party, but I hadn't brought up his name again. I hate to listen to women who whine about their love life, although I'd put up with it for years from Meredith. That's probably the reason I declined to discuss it.

"I thought it was kind of strange you never talked about him," she said. "I figured you'd lost all interest."

"I tried. But since I see him every week at my art class, it fueled the flame. Anyway, we're going out tomorrow night."

Rachel gave me a thumbs up. "Good for you."

He picked me up in his green ten-year-old truck.

"Not exactly a limo," he said as he opened the passenger door for me. "But I live on a couple of acres outside of Summerfield, and I need a truck to haul stuff around. Like you, I'm into fixing up an old house."

I questioned him about his home on the way to the restaurant.

It turned out to be a farmhouse built in the late eighteen hundreds. "But mine's a long way from being finished," he said. "In between teaching and painting and raising a son, I don't have a lot of time to spend on it. Mostly I've taken care of the essentials like plumbing and wiring. That costs an arm and a leg, and you can't even see the results."

"I can sympathize," I said.

"Yeah. My kitchen and bathroom are pretty primitive at this point. They're next on my list. But I'm not sure I can get an equity loan to do it now. Banks are sure tight with the money."

I was so glad that our renovations were all behind us and all paid off. It made me feel secure.

We both ordered pizza and beer for dinner. We discussed the class for a while and finally he got around to talking about his son.

"We might as well talk about the elephant in the room. Brian is doing well. He transferred to the culinary arts program at Weaver Academy. That got him away from those friends who were the bad influence and into something he's really interested in. I wished I'd thought of it sooner."

"Has he always liked to cook?" I asked.

"He started doing it after his mom died and discovered he really enjoyed it. It made me happy because I soon tired of frozen dinners."

"So you feel the crisis is over?" I was anxious to know the answer to this question because I knew the more he worried about his son, the less our chance of having a viable relationship.

He shrugged and looked thoughtful. "I hope so. He's still on probation so he doesn't dare get into any more trouble or he'll go to juvy. But he seems happy in school and he's made new friends there."

So it was still a tenuous situation. But at least Jay felt secure enough to invite me out.

After the movie we returned to my house.

"Won't you come in for a bit?" I asked.

"I think I'd better not this time," Jay said. "But it was a wonderful evening." He bent down and gave me a brotherly kiss on the cheek before he left.

I lay in bed for several hours afterward trying to assess the evening. He seemed interested in me though not enough to come in my house afterward. But he did say he'd better not *this time*. Did I dare hope that meant there would be another time? And the platonic kiss—what did that mean? I hoped it meant that it was difficult for him, as it was for me, to consider a new relationship after having been in a loving one for so many years. It was so hard to start all over again, especially at our age.

# CHAPTER TWELVE

Meredith called me the following Monday night.

"I talked to someone in Kiwanis about the woman at the shelter. He's an executive with a company that runs assisted living facilities. He thought he might be able to get her a job in the kitchen at one of the places."

"Would she have to cook?"

"No, I think it's more like being a dishwasher or bussing tables. I'm not real clear on what all it entails. But he said if you could get her to an interview on Friday, he'd put in a good word for her."

I took down the name and place where she was to go.

"Thanks, Meredith. I owe you one."

"This is no guarantee, Liz. But it's a possible opening."

After I hung up I realized that Samantha had no clothes suitable for a job interview. I decided to take her out shopping to buy her an outfit after I finished my stint serving breakfast that week.

On Wednesday, I sat beside Samantha as she finished her meal.

"A friend of mine has arranged for an interview at an assisted living place. It's set up for Friday. I thought I'd take you out today to find some new clothes so you'll look nice when you go."

She gave me a sardonic smile. "Look nice? Well at least I won't be wearing jeans."

That wasn't much of a display of gratitude, but I tried to put myself in her shoes. Would I be trustful of people? How would I feel if I depended on handouts? It must be mortifying to be in that position.

I took her to Friendly Shopping Center and bought her navy blue slacks and a blazer and a tailored white blouse. With her strange posture it wasn't easy to fit her, but the saleslady graciously helped us find the right sizes. She needed underwear and shoes and hose. I wanted to buy her more but she wouldn't let me.

"I don't have anywhere to keep them, and they'd probably get ripped off," she said. "In fact, I'm not so sure about what you've already bought. I only hope they're still there by Friday."

"Why don't I take them to my house, and you can get changed there before you go to the interview?"

"Okay."

That was her final word when I dropped her off. I didn't know what to make of Samantha's dismissive attitude, though I surmised it was a defensive measure after a lifetime of suffering rejection. I wondered if she would ever open up to me or show any signs of warmth or caring.

I looked forward to Thursday nights now more than ever. I'd always found it a haven for like-minded souls who loved drawing the human form. And each week I felt that my abilities were stretched just a little further, that my drawing skills were carried to a slightly higher degree and my understanding and use of color was becoming more natural to me. And now, instead of wondering whether Jay would essentially ignore me, I looked forward to taking our relationship to a higher level, God willing.

He greeted me with a warm smile but said nothing as I set up my easel and laid out my paints. Tonight we had a lovely young woman of Asian descent who posed in a Japanese robe.

Jay tried to get as many ethnic types as possible for us to paint or draw. Some of them were willing to pose nude and some were not. But I liked the challenge of painting different fabrics and the way they clung to or draped around the body. Her silk robe was a riot of color with red dominating, and I found it to be one of the more difficult sessions because I didn't want the many bright colors and patterns to overwhelm and outshine her beautiful face. Since I tend to paint everything in minute detail, I had to force myself to treat her garment in a more abstract fashion in order to emphasize her gorgeous Asian features.

I wasn't too pleased with the final result. When Jay came by I asked him what I'd done wrong.

"You just need to loosen up a bit more. Allude to the design of her robe without slavishly copying it."

"That's what I tried to do."

"You're getting there, Liz. Just keep at it."

I'd hoped he'd ask me to stay around a bit longer. But he didn't. He just smiled and winked at me as I left. I thought he'd enjoyed our date the previous weekend but maybe not. On the way home I kept going over it in my mind, wondering if I'd misinterpreted his actions. He had said he wouldn't come in my house "this time" which I supposed meant there'd be another time. Maybe he'd changed his mind since then. Or maybe he was just busy for the weekend. I had to quit dwelling on it.

The next day I picked up Samantha and took her to my house to change before going to the Fairview, the assisted living facility on Battleground Avenue where she had an appointment for an interview. She looked better in her new clothes than I'd ever seen her. But there was no denying that she was an unusual looking young woman. I realized, belatedly, that I should have arranged for her to have a haircut. I felt sure a beautician could create a hairdo that would cover her strangely placed ears and thick neck and arrange some softness around her face.

I told Samantha I'd wait in the lobby for her. A brusque older woman greeted us and took her into an office nearby. Several residents sat forlornly in wheelchairs parked against the wall while a couple of others with walkers were seated in the line of chairs that backed up to the hallway that led to the rooms. No one was talking. It was if they had simply given up on life and were waiting for the grim reaper to come for them.

I tried to engage the woman nearest me in conversation. "How do you like it here?" I asked.

"Food's awful," she said making a face. "And the place is full of old people. I don't know why I'm here."

She appeared to be about ninety. I guess that's called being in denial.

I apparently had opened the floodgates to a long list of complaints. I didn't know whether they had basis in fact or if the woman simply liked to complain. At any rate, she kept the conversation going without any help from me.

I was relieved when Samantha reappeared with the woman. "You can start a week from Monday," she was telling her. Samantha was holding paperwork to her chest.

Back in the car, she told me she'd been hired as a dishwasher. "I'll make eight-fifty an hour," she said. "I don't know if that will get me out of the shelter. Rents are so high."

"If you can get to work on the bus in the meantime, I'll see what I can do about getting you a room somewhere. That should be a lot cheaper than an apartment."

I could feel her staring at me. "You don't have to do all this, you know."

"I know that, Samantha, but I want to."

I wondered what I had gotten myself into. The next couple of days I tried to find a place for her to live. It seemed that boarding houses had gone the way of the dinosaur. I did find a couple of them on-line but when I called they had no vacancies. There didn't seem to be an apartment in town that would be affordable on her salary. How did people on low incomes get by? Apparently they lived at home or rented with several other people. Samantha didn't know anybody to make that kind of an arrangement. I had never felt such frustration.

I worried over it and prayed about it over the weekend. I'd gone this far; I couldn't back out on her now. I couldn't let her go back to the streets.

Monday morning I made the decision. I had an extra bedroom in my home that was seldom, if ever, used. I knew I had to let Samantha stay there.

I decided to wait until I saw her on Wednesday to tell her of my decision. I just didn't know what kind of a response I would get. I thought she would agree to the arrangement; surely she didn't want to be out on the streets again. But her responses to me had been so chilly, I was afraid it would be like having an unsociable stranger in the house. Most of all, I wondered how it would affect my relationship with Jay—provided there really *was* a relationship. There was nothing certain about that.

I decided to share my decision with Rachel. I was anxious to know if she thought I was out of my mind before I actually extended the invitation.

The next day we went to Elizabeth's Pizza in the Summit Shopping Center for lunch.

"I've made a huge decision," I told her, "and I want to run it by you."

"Let me guess." She gave me a knowing smile. "You're going to invite Jay to spend the night the next time you go out together."

"Oh, whoa!" I exclaimed. "We're nowhere near that yet. Besides my decision might just make that a moot point."

Her smile faded. "What on earth are you talking about?"

"Well, to begin with, I found Samantha a job."

Her smile reappeared. "That's fantastic!"

"No, not fantastic. She'll be a dishwasher in an assisted living place. It'll be a lousy job at close to minimum wage. But it's a start. I'm hoping I can eventually get her into GTCC to learn a trade."

Rachel swirled her glass of ice tea in circles on the table making the ice clink against the sides. "Is this going to get her out of the shelter?"

"No. It's not enough money. I checked out boarding houses and apartments. Do you know there are hardly any boarding houses any more? And they are full. And even teeny apartments cost more than she can afford."

"So what's she going to do?" Rachel took a swallow of tea and began chewing on the crushed ice.

"I'm going to ask her to live with me."

Rachel's mouth dropped open. She stared at me for a minute then put her hand on top of mine which was resting on the table. "I'm kind of speechless, Liz. Why are you doing this?"

How could I explain all the crazy emotions that had taunted me ever since Samantha had shown up on my doorstep? Somehow I knew that her life was intertwined with mine whether I wanted to admit it or not. I'd purposely shut down any thoughts that could negate everything I thought I knew or believed, but I couldn't deny her physical presence. She was here in Greensboro, and she desperately needed help.

I shrugged. "I just feel I have to. That's all."

She squeezed my hand. "I knew you were a good person. I just didn't know how good."

I laughed. "Oh, please. Don't make me out a martyr. I think I've lost my mind, and I'm not even sure what my motives are.

But I don't think they're entirely saintly. I may live to regret this."

I planned to take Samantha home with me after I'd finished my stint serving breakfast on Wednesday. I approached her as she was finishing her meal.

"I have something to tell you," I said as I sat down beside her.

She looked at me with curiosity but didn't say a word.

"I have an extra bedroom at my house I cleaned up for you. I'd like you to come and stay with me."

She looked a little stunned. "Why?"

"Your salary isn't going to cover the cost of an apartment anywhere. And I can't find a rooming house with a vacancy."

"You don't have to do this." For some reason she kept repeating this. Had no one ever done nice things for her before?

I couldn't figure out what she was thinking. Her face showed no emotion. Had her life experiences stripped her of the ability to feel? I knew that wasn't true because of her emotional reaction when I told her Peter was dead. Maybe these past hard months had frozen something inside her.

"I know that, Samantha. I want to. I was hoping you would come with me now."

She'd turned back to her meal, finishing the pancakes on her plate. I suppose she was pondering my proposal. I wondered if she imagined I had ulterior motives. It seemed pretty obvious that she wasn't used to people helping her out.

Finally she said, "Okay. I'll go get my things." Her enthusiasm was underwhelming.

After she'd gone back to pack her suitcase, Rachel came over to me.

"Well?"

"She's going home with me."

"How did she react?"

"As usual. With indifference. At least that's the front she puts on."

"Well," she shrugged, "it's going to be interesting."

It wasn't long before Samantha reappeared toting the bedraggled suitcase she had with her the day she first showed up at my house. It looked somewhat worse for wear. "I told them I wouldn't be back," she said.

I drove home, as usual in silence. She followed me inside carrying her suitcase as I led her to the guest room. "This will be your room," I told her. She put her suitcase on the bed and looked around but made no comment. I showed her where the guest bath was off the hall next to her room. There had been only one bathroom when we purchased the house, but we made a master bath out of what had once been a small third bedroom.

"Can I take a tub bath?" she asked. "It's been a long time since I've been in a bathtub. Showers just aren't the same."

I pulled a bottle of lavender bath crystals out from under the sink. "Here, this will make it more like a spa."

"And do you have a washer and dryer? I don't have any clean clothes."

I showed her the laundry area off the kitchen. "Feel free to use anything here. That includes food in the fridge, laundry detergent, and anything else you need."

Once I showed her where everything was including linens and kitchen utensils, I told her to make herself at home. "If I'm home and making dinner, I'll make it for the two of us. Otherwise you can make your own meals. Do you know how to cook?"

"I can make sandwiches and heat things in the microwave. My mom never taught me cooking."

"Well, I'll stock up on microwaveable meals then. But if you want to learn, I'll try and help you."

I went to the grocery and stocked up on several kinds of frozen dinners and makings for sandwiches. I generally packed a lunch to take to my studio when I wasn't going out to lunch with Rachel.

That night for dinner I fixed chili. I had her watch as I put the ingredients together since it would be an easy meal to make for herself.

"Would you write down the recipe for it?" she asked. "I think I could try to do it when I'm alone."

That little spark of interest was the most positive sign I'd had from her. Maybe a little TLC could bring her to life. If not, I guessed I could learn to live with her impassiveness.

# CHAPTER THIRTEEN

The following evening was my art class. We had a nude model, a striking young woman whose body was perfection. It was a joy to paint her even though I had trouble making her as beautiful on paper as she was in real life.

I'd been so busy worrying over Samantha, I'd almost put Jay out of my mind. But seeing him in person put him right back front and center. Since he pretty much ignored me the week before, I wasn't sure how he would act this evening. But when he came by to critique my painting he said in a low voice, "Stay around after class, won't you?" After that I thought the class would never end.

When the others had left, he said to me, "Sorry I couldn't do anything last weekend. I'd promised Brian I'd attend some school events with him. But I'm hoping you might be free tomorrow night."

I probably should have told him I'd have to consult my date book so I wouldn't seem too eager, but I was past the point of playing coy. "I just happen to have that night open in my busy social schedule," I said with a laugh so he'd know I was teasing.

"How about dinner and a little gallery hopping? It's First Friday when the art galleries are all open."

"I'd love that." I'd read about First Fridays, but I'd never participated. It wasn't something that would be fun to do alone.

Samantha was biding her time until her job started the following Monday. I'd told her to feel free to read any of the books in my house or to entertain herself by watching television. Friday morning I went with her on the bus to show her where to transfer to get to the Fairview Home on Battleground Avenue. While in the area, we went to buy her some additional pants and tops for her job.

I told her I'd be going out that evening and to help herself to any of the dinners that were in the freezer. She said she was going to try and make some chili for herself.

Jay picked me up at six. We went to Solaris restaurant just a few blocks down Summit Avenue, a great restaurant housed in what was once a garage. They specialized in Spanish tapas, and I ordered the Spanish Orchards plate with assorted cheeses, fruit, olives and crackers. Jay tried the artichoke and spinach hummus and fried pickles, and we enjoyed trying each other's food since the point of tapas is sharing. We knew there would be food at the galleries as well so we ate lightly.

After eating we began the gallery visits at the Cultural Arts Center only a block away. There were five galleries at the center so we spent considerable time there. Earl had paintings of jazz musicians at the African-American Atelier, and he was there to greet the guests. I loved his paintings, which were done in bold strokes with bright poster-like colors. They exuded joy and energy.

He greeted us enthusiastically, and he and Jay engaged in shop talk while I roamed the gallery and nibbled on hors d'oeuvres. Like I needed more to eat.

From there we went to Green Hill Gallery, the largest and most prestigious in the center.

"I have a surprise for you," Jay said as we entered through the gift shop.

"What?"

"You'll see."

He took my hand and led me to the far wall. There two giant canvases hung, both featuring young women seated languidly, one on a couch, one on a chaise longue, dressed discreetly in flowing dresses. I recognized the models from my art class, but I didn't recognize the style of the painter. The paintings were done in what I'd call a cross between realism and impressionism with just enough detail to make them come alive yet enough looseness to invoke the sense of the personality contained within. The paintings were absolutely striking.

"Who . . . ?" I started to ask.

He led me closer to the first painting and pointed to the signature in the lower right hand corner: "Kadlacek."

I'd never seen his work before. He never displayed it at the art class, and now I could see why. It would either inspire or totally intimidate the students.

"My god, Jay. Those are beautiful. I had no idea you were such a wonderful painter!"

He laughed. "Had I given the impression I was second rate because of my teaching style?"

"Oh, no. Not at all. I'm just surprised you've never let the students see your work."

"I want everyone to develop their own style. I don't want them to copy me. That's why I give you so much freedom in class."

"Well, now, I'm really embarrassed to show you my pathetic attempts."

His smile quickly vanished. "Listen here, Liz. I don't want to hear that kind of talk. You've only begun to treat your painting seriously, and you have a lot of talent. You should never denigrate your abilities."

What a dear, sweet man. I didn't know if he was telling the truth, but I loved hearing it. No wonder he was so successful as a teacher.

We spent the next several hours walking around the downtown area to visit all the open galleries. Jay knew the owners and the featured artists at almost every stop. It was like old home week to him. It was such fun to be a part of it.

When the galleries closed, I invited him to come to my house for a drink. I knew Samantha would probably be up, and that was certain to put a cramp in our style, but I wanted Jay to know she was there. If he couldn't deal with the fact I had her rooming with me, I wanted to know it sooner rather than later. I felt I needed to warn him of her presence however.

"I have someone staying with me for the time being," I told him as we drove toward my house.

He glanced over at me, disappointment showing in his expression. "Oh?"

I didn't want to go into detail, not wanting him to prejudge her on the fact of her homelessness. "It's till she gets on her feet."

He said nothing else on the short drive.

I could see the lights on in the living room. I'd secretly hoped that Samantha had already gone to bed and left the lights on for my sake. But when I opened the door, I saw her sitting on the couch watching television still clothed in what she had been wearing that day. She looked startled when she realized I had a man with me.

I introduced them to each other, all the while watching Jay's face for any sign of a reaction to her strange appearance. But he was his usual charming self.

Samantha, on the other hand, seemed to retreat into herself and barely acknowledged him. "It's my bedtime," she declared, and hurried out of the living room.

"Have a seat, Jay," I said gesturing toward the couch. "What can I get you? A beer? Wine? Soft drink?" My voice sounded normal, but my insides were trembling. Would he stay just long enough not to be rude and then escape? Did the fact of Samantha being there rule out any romantic involvement? Our relationship was so new and fragile that I worried that this could be the obstruction to derail it altogether.

"A beer would be good," he said.

I retreated to the kitchen, got two cold beers out of the fridge and opened a bag of pretzels, dumping them into a bowl. We'd snacked so much at the galleries I didn't think he'd want much to eat.

I settled onto the other end of the couch, close enough to be friendly but not so close as to seem predatory. I knew that young women were more often than not the ones who initiated intimacy, but I was from another generation and I couldn't get used to the idea.

"So, Liz," Jay said, after a swallow of beer, "I feel you know a lot more about me than I do about you. I want to hear your life's story."

"Well, I can do that in about two sentences. Mostly it's pretty dull."

"Go for it."

"I grew up in Greensboro, went to UNCG, met my husband there, and got married soon after graduation. We bought this house fifteen years ago after living in Guilford Hills, and, as I told you, spent years fixing it up ourselves."

"And doing a beautiful job of it," he said, waving his beer around to encompass the room. "Did you ever work outside the house?"

"I worked in the office of a jewelry store for some years. Pretty boring over all."

"No kids?"

"That was a very touchy point. We tried for years but without any luck."

"That must have been hard." His face showed genuine

sympathy. Perhaps it was his creative nature, but he had extraordinary empathy for a man.

"And how did your husband die?"

"Leukemia. He was sick for seven months."

"My wife had ovarian cancer. That's about how long she lasted. I know what you went through." He moved over closer to me and took my hand. "We're both relatively young, Liz. We still have many years left to us. Life has to go on."

In spite of myself, I began to cry. "I know, I know. I'm working really hard on that."

He pulled me close to him in a hug. "How about we work on it together?"

Then he tilted my head up with his finger under my chin and looked into my eyes with longing. "I think we both need affection to fill up that dark hole that has been ripped in our hearts." He then kissed me tenderly but with unmistakable desire, stroking my hair like a child would pet a kitten. I almost felt like purring in response.

Then he released me. "Under the circumstances," he said, giving a nod toward the bedroom wing, "I think I must leave now. But how about coming to my house next weekend?" His face broke into a conspiratorial grin. "Maybe you can advise me on some remodeling projects I'd like to do. Brian is going to visit his grandparents in Morganton."

I knew exactly what he meant, and I was torn between desire and fear. Was it too soon? Certainly not by today's standards. I'd lived a very sheltered life as Peter had been my only lover. But I did so want to know this man better, this gentle man with the enormous talent.

"Sounds good to me," I said though I had all sorts of reservations. But an inner voice was telling me *go for it.*

"How about I pick you up at six on Friday. I think I'll fix a meal for you. Brian has gotten me more interested in cooking, and he's shown me some really cool recipes."

"I'd love that." Peter had spoiled me by cooking most of our dinners and I'd missed that a lot.

Sunday Meredith called and asked me to meet her for dinner at the Grandover Resort, a luxurious hotel that's the centerpiece of the development where she lives.

"I was wondering what happened with the job opportunity I called you about," she said as she attacked her salad.

"I'm sorry, Meredith. I should have called you. Samantha is starting there for work tomorrow. Thanks for setting it up."

"Have you been able to find her housing yet?" She speared a cherry tomato off the salad and plopped it into her mouth.

I was reluctant to tell Meredith because I knew how she would react. "She's staying with me."

She stared at me, her fork with another tomato on it poised in midair. "Are you out of your mind? You don't know anything about her. What if she steals from you?"

"Good god, Meredith, you are such a cynic."

"I may be a cynic, but you are a Goody Two Shoes. Peter would be horrified to know what you've done."

"I don't think so." I was beginning to lose my cool.

"Why are you doing this, Liz?" She had put her fork down in order to lean over and engage me with her portentous stare.

"Because there's no place out there she can afford to rent. I can't let her go out on the streets again."

She sank back in her chair, unable to come up with a retort. We sat in silence for several minutes munching on our salads.

Finally, just to start up the conversation again I said, "So what's happening with you?"

She blinked and a faint blush rose in her cheeks. "Well . . . , I know I said I'd sworn off men forever. . . ."

"Like I really believed that?" I laughed at her discomfort. I don't think I'd ever seen Meredith blush before. This must be something!

"A lawyer representing a company that needed patent work came to our office a couple of weeks ago. I'd only just met him the last time I talked to you. But he invited me out and . . . do you believe in love at first sight?"

"Meredith! You've been married three times and gone out with so many men I can't count them. And you're asking *me?*"

She actually looked embarrassed, another first. "I think I've been in lust at first sight, but not love. I guess I had the two confused."

"So what makes you think this is different?"

She looked into the distance with a dreamy smile. "He's so sweet and considerate. I guess I always went for the macho men before. Carl is different. At least at this point he seems different. I just pray I'm not wrong about him."

"Well I hope so, too." Meredith had had enough grief; she didn't need any more disappointments. I was so tempted to tell her about Jay and next weekend, but I managed to keep silent. After her tirade when I told her he decided to concentrate on Brian's problems, I didn't want to hear anything negative out of her.

She spent most of the meal raving about Carl's many attributes, and I was satisfied to say little and pretend to listen. Actually I was mostly lost in my own thoughts about Jay and our relationship.

When we parted, she hugged me and said, "Liz, you really need to find someone. It'll make such a difference in your life."

I nodded and agreed with her. "You're probably right, Meredith; you're probably right."

# CHAPTER FOURTEEN

I got up early the next morning to make a filling breakfast for Samantha. I didn't plan to make a habit of it, but I thought it would be nice to send her off on her first day of work with a substantial meal. I cooked scrambled eggs and bacon and even grits which I served with toast, orange juice and coffee.

"Can you show me how to make the eggs and grits?" Samantha asked as she wolfed them down. I could see that my food bill would be rising considerably, but I didn't mind; it was good to see she had a healthy appetite. I didn't know if she would be getting any meals at work; I'd forgotten to ask the day she had her interview.

I thought about her most of the day as I painted in my studio, wondering how she was faring. I had no idea what I would do next if she hated it so much she quit or if they fired her. Now that she was in my house I could scarcely kick her out again. But I didn't want someone there who lived off my dole indefinitely and didn't try to improve her own circumstances. It could turn into a very sticky situation. The more I thought about it, the more uneasy I became.

She didn't get home until eight in the evening. She looked so exhausted it alarmed me.

"How did it go?" I asked her.

She was heading straight to her room. "Okay, I guess," she said, sounding as if it were not okay at all.

"Have you eaten?" I asked as she rounded the corner into the hall.

"Yeah." Then I heard her bedroom door close.

I sat there wondering what to do. If she'd been my child, I would have gone to her door and knocked and begged her to let me in. But she wasn't my child; she was practically a stranger. I decided there was nothing I could do until she decided to confide in me, if ever. All I could do was try to make her time in my home as pleasant as possible.

But I saw very little of her after that. By the next morning when I got up to fix her breakfast, she informed me she could get her own and all she wanted was cereal and coffee anyway. And every evening she went directly to her room, barely speaking as she passed through the living room.

Wednesday morning Rachel and I served meals as usual at Urban Ministry. I hadn't had a chance to talk to her since Samantha had come to live with me.

"So how's it going?" she asked as she spooned a large helping of grits onto a plate.

"It's hard to say. I rarely see her."

"What do you mean?"

"She stays in her room a lot, and since she started work on Monday, I've only seen her as she walks through the living room in the evening and goes straight to her bedroom. I can hardly get a grunt out of her."

"Well, I expect she's exhausted at the end of the day."

"I think it's more than that. I suspect she hates the job. And who wouldn't? If only she could get some training to get a decent job."

"She's a grown woman, Liz. She's going to have to make her own decisions. You can't take over her life for her." She looked at me with great seriousness.

That hurt. I was only trying to help, not "take over."

"I'm not going to force her to do anything. I just thought she might need some help to get started. She doesn't know our area at all."

Rachel seemed to realize she'd upset me. She put her arm around my shoulder. "You're an amazing woman, Liz. Very few people would have taken her in the way you did. I think it would be fine if you show her what her options might be. The rest is up to her."

"It's part selfishness too. What can I do if she quits her job and can't or won't get another? I can't support her forever. I don't want her in my home indefinitely. I feel like I've gotten myself into something I may have a whole lot of trouble getting out of."

Rachel pulled at her ear in thought. I could tell she didn't have an answer to that. "I'm sure things will work out. And, by the way, what's happening with you and Jay?"

I knew the last was an attempt to change an unpleasant subject. I wasn't quite ready to share my mixed emotions with anyone. So I smiled, enigmatically I hoped, and said, "It's coming along."

On Thursday night at art class we had a young black man who posed in street clothes—low-riding baggy pants, unlaced expensive athletic shoes and a T-shirt with Snoop Dog's face displayed in a psychedelic fashion. His skin was so dark it literally shone like patent leather and his dreadlocks stood out like a halo around his head. It was the most challenging model we'd had since I'd been in the class. Capturing his skin tones without making his head look like a black hole was very difficult.

Jay came by as I was choosing colors for his face.

"Don't use too much black," he warned. "Solid black simply goes 'dead.' Use dark umbers, siennas, violets, greens, oranges and blues. These can give you deep, rich tones that capture the sheen of the skin."

He took my palette, mixed some paints together and dabbed them on a scrap piece of paper. "See, this is how you do it."

He winked at me as he handed the palette back.

By the end of the evening, I was pleased with my painting. Every week I thanked God that I enrolled in this class, not only because I met Jay, but also because I was learning so much about painting which enriched my life more each day.

As I was packing away my watercolors and brushes, Jay walked by and whispered in my ear, "I'll pick you up at six tomorrow. Can't wait."

I smiled a secret smile all to myself. I couldn't wait either.

The next morning I got up when Samantha was eating her breakfast. I sat down across from her at the dining table.

"I'll be out of town this weekend," I said. Technically Summerfield was out of town but just barely. "I had an extra house key made for you, and there's plenty of frozen dinners in the fridge."

I laid the key on the table next to her plate. A brief flicker of what looked like fear showed momentarily on her face, and then her normal blank expression returned.

"Is everything all right?" I asked, not really expecting an answer.

She continued to eat her cereal but her brows knitted, and I could tell she was trying hard not to cry.

"What is it, Samantha?"

"Nothing," she said in a strangled voice.

"It can't be nothing." I knew I sounded impatient, but I was tired of trying to drag two words out of her.

"They hate me. They make fun of me. They say I'm in the Dish Pit and that's where I belong because I'm the pits." I could tell she was barely holding it together.

I felt a burning ache deep inside me and a desire to go punch somebody's lights out. Why are people so cruel?

"I don't know why people act that way, but there are always some who act like jerks no matter where you work," I said. "You just have to try and ignore them. Do your job as best you can, and maybe they'll promote you into something better."

"Like what? Bussing tables? Big deal." I'd never heard Samantha sound so angry. But for the first time I saw a spark in her eyes. Always before her whole demeanor signaled surrender, abandonment of hope. But this miserable job had lit a fire under her. Maybe that wasn't such a bad thing.

"If you can hang in there for a while, we could explore getting you into Guilford Tech next fall if you're interested."

She looked up at me appearing distraught. "I'm not smart enough."

"I don't believe that for a minute, Samantha. Don't put yourself down that way."

I wasn't sure just how capable she would be of taking courses on that level, but I felt there had to be something that would suit her.

She busied herself eating the rest of her breakfast and was disinclined to talk about it any more.

As promised, Jay pulled into my driveway just before six that evening in his truck. He came to the door, and when I answered it, he bowed and said, "Your limo has arrived."

I had packed a weekend bag which was just inside the door, so I replied, "Let's hit the road then."

We rode in companionable silence in his truck over to Wendover and on to Battleground Avenue which led out of town toward Summerfield. It was mid March, and although the trees were still bare, a haze of red in the maples and tiny buds along the branches of the tulip poplars promised spring was very near.

We drove past Lake Higgins and Lake Brandt, through the countryside which was swiftly being overtaken by development. Soon we took a right and were onto side roads unknown to me. A few twists and turns and we pulled into a gravel driveway. An old house sat well back from the road, its front yard a heavily wooded area with a small patch of green lawn. It was a typical farmhouse, rectangular, two stories high, with a front porch spanning its width. Green metal roofs graced the house and the porch and appeared much newer than the gray siding that must have been white at one time. The house didn't appear to be in great need of repair, just some loving care and fresh paint.

Jay came around and opened the truck door for me and helped me out, pulling my suitcase from behind the seat. He ushered me through the front door and directly into the living room. It was a big, boxy room with large windows that faced west and spread the light of the dying sun across the wide plank floor. A stone fireplace at the far end of the room looked as if it had been used a lot because smoke had stained the rocks above the opening with a blue-black glaze. The room was sparsely furnished with what appeared to be hand-me-down furniture of various styles and periods. The only hint of elegance was the many paintings by Jay in vivid colors, some of models, some landscapes.

"Let me show you your room," he said as he gestured toward the stairs to the left.

*My* room? What exactly did that mean? Was this going to be a chaste weekend after all, and I had misjudged him?

I followed him up the steps and down the hall to a bedroom at the far end on the front of the house. It had a double bed, an oak dresser at least a century old, and a chair in the corner. The bed was covered with an old handmade quilt. There were more of Jay's paintings on the walls.

"The bathroom is just across the hall and down one door,"

109

he said putting down my suitcase. "If you'd like to freshen up, I'll be downstairs fixing dinner."

I nodded, and he left to go downstairs. I was confused now. Was this a romantic rendezvous or not? Had I read too much into his invitation?

I used the bathroom and then decided to explore the other upstairs rooms. There were two besides my bedroom and the bath. I looked into the first and saw that it had to be Brian's room since it was filled with posters of rock and sports stars. It had the usual teen mess of clothes and school books and unidentifiable objects piled everywhere.

The last room I looked into had to be Jay's bedroom. An army blanket covered a mattress and box spring next to a small table with an old pottery lamp. The only other piece of furniture was an ancient desk that held a laptop. If there had ever been feminine touches they were long gone. I closed the door again—I didn't want him to know I was snooping—and went downstairs.

Jay was in the kitchen behind the living room. It was a big room, one that probably had been remodeled in the 1950s with knotty pine cabinets, an ugly yellow electric stove, and a small refrigerator. A splayed-leg maple table with two captains' chairs was in the center of the room on the worn green linoleum. It had already been set with silverware and wine goblets on red vinyl placemats with white cloth napkins, and there were four mismatched candlesticks in the center with tall white tapers.

Jay was standing at the stove tending a skillet. "I made the salad in advance, and I put potatoes in the oven to bake."

"So what's in the skillet?" I asked.

"Chicken scaloppini with piccata sauce."

"That sounds complicated."

"Not really. Brian taught me how to make it. It's just sautéed cutlets topped with parsley and lemon sauce."

"Don't give away any secrets. Make your guests think you've slaved over it half the day."

"I'll remember that. Why don't you go ahead and sit down. It's almost ready. What kind of wine would you like?"

"I'm no wine connoisseur. About all I know is that there's red wine and white wine and I usually prefer white. Why don't you choose for me?"

"Okay. I've kind of gotten into North Carolina wines. You know they are making some really good ones in our state. I have a 2008 Surry Community College Petit Manseng, a nice white. Their viticulture program is one of the few on the east coast that uses the Manseng grape, which comes from Spain and France."

"I had no idea they were making wine at the community colleges."

"They're working hard in this state to replace the tobacco crop as it becomes less and less viable."

Jay turned down the heat under the skillet and pulled a bottle of wine from the refrigerator which he uncorked and poured into the goblets on the table. Then he retrieved a lighter from a drawer and lit the four candles. He held up the lighter and grinned. "A remnant of my smoking days. Glad that's behind me."

He dished up the chicken onto plates, added baked potatoes from the oven and pulled two bowls of salad from the refrigerator. "Hope oil and vinegar suit you."

"Perfect," I said.

He sat down, picked up his wine glass and held it high. "Let's toast to a new relationship."

I raised mine and clicked it against his. The resulting sound was like the opening note of a brand new melody.

# CHAPTER FIFTEEN

After dinner Jay took me outside to a large storage building behind the house that had been modified for a painting studio. Several skylights, where now a shred of moonlight cast pools of pale gold on the floor, would give ample light during the day in addition to a bank of windows on the north side. Piles of blank and partially finished canvasses leaned against the walls, and an empty easel stood before a platform where models could pose. A huge battered table held paints, jars of brushes, bottles of turpentine and linseed oil, rags and other paraphernalia. A dorm-sized fridge was in a far corner.

"Do you always use oils when you paint here?" I asked.

"I switch between oil and watercolor. I like to use watercolor sometimes because it dries fast and is less messy."

"But it's almost more challenging, isn't it?" I felt that way because I struggled with it constantly. I'd never attempted to use oils.

"In many ways, yes. You can make some changes to watercolor if you don't like what you've done, but once it's down, that's pretty much it. With oil you can keep working it over and over. It's more forgiving."

"Maybe I should try it."

"You're doing well with watercolors. I say keep on with that. At least for now."

I wondered if he really meant that or if it was a kind of cerebral foreplay. Either way I'd take it.

We returned to the house, and Jay built a fire in the fireplace, put on a CD of Schumann love songs, and offered me another glass of wine. Since I was a bit on the uptight side at this point, I readily agreed.

We talked about our lives, the painting class and whatever else came into our minds. I had a sense that Jay was a little nervous too.

"Why don't we put on some dance music?" he asked finally.

"Sounds good," I said. But truthfully I was somewhat alarmed. Peter had never enjoyed dancing, said he had two left feet. So it had been many years since I'd danced, in fact not since college. Was I about to make a fool of myself?

Jay spent some time sorting through his stack of CDs until he finally held one up.

"This would be good." He slid it into the CD player and then came over and held out his arms.

The sound of "My Eyes Adored You," by Frankie Valli filled the room with its sweet nostalgic strains. Talk about going back in time.

I stood up. "I've got to warn you. It's been years and years since I've done this."

He smiled. "Just follow me." He then folded me into his embrace and began to sway to the music. I willed myself to relax, to give myself up to the moment and enjoy it. The wine certainly helped.

In only minutes I felt completely at ease, moving to Jay's confident lead. Before I realized it, we were cheek to cheek, feeling the sweet notes surround us as we gracefully, thanks to Jay, moved about the floor. When the song ended, he didn't let go but pulled me closer and tipped up my head with his finger. He looked steadily into my eyes for a minute or two, then leaned in and kissed me. Passionately.

I had anticipated the moment many times before that

evening. But it surpassed anything my imagination could conjure up. His lips were both rough and tender, and waves of long suppressed emotion flooded through me. Maybe my heart hadn't entirely shriveled up after all.

Without a word he took my hand and led me toward the stairs. We climbed them together holding hands. Leading me down the hall to my bedroom, he drew me gently toward the bed. We sat on the edge together as he kissed me again, his hands caressing my body as if he were assessing each curve and plane for a painting. I began to unbutton my blouse, and he took over the task, pulling it off and unhooking my bra.

"You are so lovely," he whispered as his hands moved over me slowly and gently sending waves of desire through me. I thought I might never again experience such pleasure, but how wrong I was.

Peter had been a good lover, but he had the soul of a businessman: deliberate and steady and unimaginative. Jay was an artist, and he made love the way he painted—with passion and flair but leavened with tenderness. He did not rush me but followed my lead as though he and I were working together to create a beautiful piece of art.

We made love several times that night, and Jay aroused sensibilities in me that I didn't know I had. When we had exhausted ourselves, I lay awake in the darkness wondering what I had gotten myself into. Was I truly ready for a whole new chapter in my life? Or, at my age, should I just have accepted the status quo? I had never imagined my life would take a detour into a whole new world at this point in time.

Jay fixed an elaborate breakfast the next morning. He made an omelet with cheese, bacon bits, green peppers and onions. He also fried up some potatoes and made a fruit bowl with cut up melons and pineapple.

"For a guy who doesn't cook much, you surprise me," I said as I dug in.

"That's Brian's influence. He likes to show me what he's learned in class."

"Am I ever going to meet Brian?" I knew this was a tricky question because it implied that I was more than a one night stand. I wanted to make sure that was his intention.

Jay seemed to be pondering this as he took several sips of coffee. "Yes, I do want you to meet him. But I have to prepare him for the idea first. He seems to be turning his life around, and I don't want to do anything too fast to jeopardize that."

It really hurt to think that he saw me as an impediment to his son's progress. Did he think Brian would see me as some kind of monster? I know it's especially difficult for teenagers who have lost a mother or father to accept the fact that their surviving parent is interested in someone new. But did that mean Jay had to put his life on hold indefinitely? It seemed so unfair. To both of us.

I held my tongue, but it was difficult.

Jay must have seen something in my face that told him how I felt. He reached out and took my hand. "That doesn't mean we can't see each other you know. I just want to hold off on introducing you two."

I nodded. "I understand." But that didn't mean I was happy about it.

As we washed up the dishes Jay said, "Do you know what I want to do today?"

"Give me a hint."

"Think of Thursday evenings."

"You want to have a painting class?"

"Not quite. I want to paint and have you as my model."

"You're kidding."

"I'm serious. And I want you to pose without clothes."

115

I couldn't believe my ears. Had the man lost his mind? "Jay, for god's sake, I'm fifty-six years old. You don't want to paint me like that."

"Why not?"

"Because . . . my bod ain't what it used to be for one thing. For another, what if Brian sees it after he has met me? I'd die of embarrassment."

Jay put down the towel he'd been using to dry dishes and pulled me into his arms.

"Don't put yourself down that way. It's not just young girls who have beautiful bodies; women of any age can be attractive. Think of the women the great masters have painted. They're usually not pubescent girls. You are quite lovely, Liz, and I would consider it a privilege to paint you."

"I'm flattered. But you haven't answered my question about Brian."

"Brian never comes out to the studio. And I shall keep it covered. I just want to do this for myself. I have no intention of displaying it."

"Are you sure about this, Jay?"

"Very sure."

We finished the dishes in silence. I was trying to think of all the reasons I should say no. Was this going to turn out to be something like teens did with "sexting"? Use a nude picture for revenge one day? Could Jay possibly use this against me in the future? I was appalled at myself for being so distrustful. I couldn't believe he was anything other than he appeared—a caring, thoughtful, vastly talented man. But today's world made one suspicious of just about everything.

I decided that life was just too short to be so fearful. I had to take chances now and then or my life would be stagnant and sterile.

As we hung up the dish towels I said, "Okay. I guess I can do that. Please don't hang me out to dry, Jay."

He bent over and kissed me. "Never."

Thankfully his studio had a good heating system because it was a blustery March day. But the sun was shining and the light coming through the skylights and windows helped warm it up. It was a much more cheerful place than it had been the night before.

I waited while Jay set up his canvas and prepared his palette. He had a pile of materials on a stool in one corner, and he pulled out an old paisley shawl that he spread on the platform.

"Okay, I'm ready for you," he said.

Although he'd seen me without clothes the night before, that was in the throes of passion. Now I turned my back to him modestly as I stepped out of my jeans, sweater and underwear. In this light, bright room I felt embarrassed. Finally I turned around, foolishly trying to cover myself with my hands.

He tipped his head to one side and grinned broadly. "You need to accept the fact that you have a lovely body and not try to hide it."

I put my hands down to my sides but still stood stiffly and ill at ease.

"Come here, Liz," he said beckoning me with his hand. "Come lie down on this shawl."

I did as he said. But I didn't know what to do with my head.

"Wait a sec," he said. He went back to the corner and after rummaging through a pile, pulled out a large square pillow covered in a zebra-skin print. He came over and put it beneath my head. "Lie back on this." As I did, he asked, "Is that comfortable?"

I nodded.

"Okay, bend your legs a little and half turn toward me. There now. Put your left hand beneath the pillow. Okay. That looks good."

At first I was so tense I could feel little muscle spasms in my legs, and my stomach felt as if I might even upchuck. But as the morning wore on, I became more relaxed and decided I would just think of it as a prolonged rest period. I tried to think of pleasant things, of sunny days and flower gardens, whatever would take my mind off the fact I was lying there naked in front of him.

Jay studied me intently and began to paint with broad strokes. I was extremely curious to see what he was doing. During the breaks he offered me a robe he obviously kept there for other models, and we'd sit on the edge of the platform drinking beers from the fridge, but he wouldn't let me see the painting.

"Wait till I'm further along," he said. "I won't be able to finish it today, but I should have a good foundation by noon. Then I'll let you see."

It was almost twelve thirty when he said, "Okay. It's been a long session. You're a very good model, Liz. You keep very still."

"It helped you put me in a comfortable pose. Now I want a peek."

He handed me the robe. "Come. It's far from done, but you can get an idea."

When I saw the portrait, I was filled with joy instead of the embarrassment I'd expected. He had depicted me not as some idealized woman, which would have been out of touch with reality, but had rendered my flaws so sympathetically that I could feel the empathy and love that had gone into the painting. This was a portrait of a real woman not a mannequin, and I felt he had captured my very essence.

I could feel my eyes tear up. "It's beautiful, Jay. I think you found the inner me." I tried to laugh to hide my emotions.

"I think you'll like it even better when I'm done. I'm far enough along now that I can finish it without you having to pose."

"You'll let me see the final product."

"Of course."

"But no one else."

He laughed. "I already promised that. You do believe me, don't you?"

"Sure." I'd gone this far. It was too late for any reservations.

# CHAPTER SIXTEEN

He looked at his watch. "It's almost one o'clock. Why don't we go out to lunch?"

"Good idea. I don't know why, but I've developed quite an appetite. It's not like I was expending any energy lying on that platform all morning." I took off the robe, this time without feeling embarrassed, and put my clothes back on. Jay was cleaning off his brushes.

"If you can hold off a half an hour or so, I'd like to go to Kernersville."

"Why there?" Kernersville was a small town about twenty miles west of Greensboro on Highway 40.

"Ever hear of Körner's Folly?"

"Sure. I've always wanted to see it but somehow never got there."

"I thought it would be a fun afternoon. We'll grab a bite at one of the restaurants in town, then do the tour."

We took Route 150 out of Summerfield through the little town of Oak Ridge, the centerpiece of which was a military academy that was under siege from the bad economy, and on into Kernersville, named after the grandfather of the man who built Körner's Folly.

We had lunch at Cagney's where we ordered personal-sized pizzas, ham and pineapple for Jay and mushroom and green pepper for me.

Körner's Folly was just down the street, a square brick

Gothic-style house with steep roof peaks on all four sides that has been labeled "The Strangest House in the World." I could almost envision the Addams family living there. With twenty-two rooms on seven levels, it's almost like a funhouse. There's a room with a ceiling height of just five feet seven inches as well as a grand reception, and theater rooms with soaring ceilings.

The builder, Jule Körner, was a talented man, an artist and interior designer as well as an advertising man who lived in the late eighteen hundreds. At one time he worked for one of the tobacco companies and conceived of iconic signs of a bull that he painted on every conceivable surface all over the Southeast and beyond: barns, roofs, mountainsides, any place that he could find. It is known as the most successful advertising campaign in American history. Gifted with a droll sense of humor, he painted bulls as large as eighty by one hundred and fifty feet. Some were so anatomically correct that they garnered much publicity. It is said he would drum up attention for the paintings by writing letters complaining about the images to editors himself. Then he would correct the problem with strategic additions.

At the same time he built a small home and connecting stable that would serve as a showroom for his interior decorating business carried on under his pseudonym Reubin Rink. This is the core of Körner's Folly.

When the management of the tobacco company wanted him to move to New York City promising to make him a millionaire, he refused. He was born and bred a Tar Heel and he wouldn't leave the state.

When he married, his wife Alice turned down his offer to build her a mansion, saying instead they should expand his bachelor pad. And so Körner's Folly was born. He called it that, in fact memorializing the name in tile on the front porch when the local gossips called him crazy for investing one hundred thousand dollars in the construction.

The house was completed in 1880, though he never stopped refining it as a showcase for his interior design. Every piece of woodwork, the painted and embossed ceilings, and each of the fifteen fireplaces are unique.

It was during this renovation that the many levels and varied ceiling heights were added. What had originally been a carriageway between the house and stables became the foyer and dining room. The living room became the master bedroom with stairs up to the low-ceilinged children's playroom complete with interior window where their mother could keep an eye on them. I climbed the stairs to look around but Jay knew it would be impossible for him to stand upright under its ceiling that was only five feet seven inches high, so he waited for me below.

We took the self-guided tour through the home, amazed and delighted by the original furnishings Jule designed, including a three-way chair that was in a circle so that each seat faced outward in a different direction.

"It would be pretty hard to carry on a conversation in this without getting a crick in your neck trying to converse with the person behind you," I said.

"Yeah," agreed Jay. "Maybe it was meant for antisocial people."

When we reached the upstairs reception room, we admired the beautiful murals painted on and near the ceiling in the huge room.

"Jule was a talented artist as well as a designer," Jay said. "This room was originally his studio, but after he got married they used it for entertaining."

"Oh, look," I said, reading the description of the room, "those are little 'kissing corners' beside each of the two fireplaces. Apparently, Jule liked to defy convention and made these curtained alcoves so that engaged or married couples could smooch out of sight."

"Well, I think we ought to try one out."

He took my hand and pulled me into the nearest one. It was very shallow, and we barely fit. He pulled me to him and kissed me with exuberance. With his talent and joie de vivre, I thought Jay could very well have been Jule reincarnated.

The top floor, once used as a billiard room and ballroom, was later converted into a theater after the two Körner children, Gilmer and Dore, were born. Their mother began a Juvenile Lyceum where she gave local children the opportunity to write and perform, and the theater was created when the group outgrew the reception room. It was still used by the local community theater group.

Since the irregular ceiling that follows the peaked roof line is covered with paintings of cupids, it is referred to as "Cupid's Park." I wondered if Jay had known the name of it and had brought me here in a moment of romantic inspiration. Probably not, I decided, but still I embraced the possibility.

It's nearly impossible to adequately describe this intriguing house and its many rooms in various shapes and sizes. It's obvious that a highly talented and imaginative man with great wit was behind it all.

We left the main house, passed by the deteriorated outhouse built of brick to duplicate the shape of the main house, another humorous touch, to the cottage where "Aunt Dealy," the beloved former slave and nanny to Jule and his children lived. When Aunt Dealy died, the local Moravian cemetery refused to allow her to be buried there. So Jule bought some adjoining land so she could be interred next to his family.

"I wish I could have known this man," I said to Jay as we drove away.

"Me, too," Jay said. "He not only was extremely talented but apparently a stand up kind of guy."

Yes, I thought, a lot like you.

As we drove back to Summerfield the sky darkened and the wind picked up.

"Looks like we're going to get a downpour," Jay said as the first sprinkles hit the windshield. By the time we reached his house, the storm was full blown. The thunder and lightning were carrying on like Liszt's "Totendanz," and the walkway from the drive to the house appeared to be several inches under water.

"Don't get out just yet," Jay said as he turned off the ignition. He jumped out of the truck, ran around the front, and opened my door. "I'm going to carry you in. No sense in both of us getting soaked shoes."

He picked me up as if I weighed nothing, in spite of his spare frame, and ran to the front door which was covered by the porch roof. He set me down while he unlocked the door. Then he picked me up again and carried me into the living room.

"Just thought I'd try a practice run," he said as he put me down gently onto the sofa.

I was so taken aback I didn't know what to say.

Jay got busy and started a fire in the fireplace. Though I only got a little wet, its warmth felt good. Jay took off his soaked shoes and socks and we sat side by side and quietly watched the flames flicker and dance. I thought of the many fireplaces in Körner's Folly and wondered if the couple made love in front of any of them.

Jay must have read my mind. Before I knew it, he brought a blanket from upstairs and laid it on the floor in front of the fireplace. The rest of the evening was bliss. He was an artist not only in putting paint to canvas but in making love.

# CHAPTER SEVENTEEN

Sunday morning we lingered in bed, content to lie in each other's arms. Finally Jay said, "I'm going to fix us brunch. Brian will be coming home sometime this afternoon so I'm afraid I'll have to take you home after we eat."

I didn't want this lovely weekend to end, but I knew it must.

Jay made crepes with mushrooms and served them with orange and grapefruit sections, sourdough bread toast, and coffee.

I reluctantly packed up my things after we cleaned up the kitchen and wondered when I would be able to return. The sky was dark, and it looked like rain was imminent—again.

On the way home Jay brought up Samantha. "You know, you've not said much about her at all. Why is she living with you?" I wondered if he was thinking the same thing I was: as long as Samantha was at my house and Brian was living with Jay, our chance of having a rendezvous like this weekend was slim.

I didn't want to go into too much detail. "You know I help serve breakfast at Urban Ministry on Wednesday mornings. Samantha was there, and I found out that she was living at the shelter after being on the streets. I knew she couldn't stay there indefinitely, so I thought I might be able to help her."

"You really have a big heart, you know that?" he said. "Not many people would be willing to take a stranger in."

I shrugged. "I didn't intend to have her stay with me. I arranged to get her a job and thought she could find a place to rent. But the reality is she doesn't make enough money to rent any place. I felt I had to help her out till she could get on her own two feet. I'm hoping she can eventually learn a skill where she can support herself."

"What is she doing now?"

"Working as a dishwasher in an assisted living place."

"Oh, god," Jay said glancing over at me, "I can't imagine anything worse."

"I think sleeping on the streets would be worse."

"I can't argue that. You know, I forgot to tell you. I was intrigued by her appearance when I saw her at your place. People's faces are my line of work; I have never seen anyone quite like Samantha."

"I think that has been her cross to bear. She told me kids always made fun of her at school. And though she's barely talked about her job, I think they are giving her a hard time there. Life is more difficult when your looks are unusual. I don't know why people are so cruel to anyone who's different."

"Well, I decided to go on line and see if I could figure out just what caused her anomalies. It took me a while to put it all together, but I eventually found out that there is a name for what she has. It's called Noonan Syndrome."

It felt as though a knife had been thrust through my heart, and I was struck dumb. My worst fears had been realized, fears that I had continually pushed to the back of my mind so I wouldn't have to consider them. But now I had to face facts: Samantha had to be Peter's child. I couldn't deny it. The probability that there could be any other answer was almost nil. When we underwent so many tests when I was trying to get pregnant, we learned that Peter carried the gene for Noonan syndrome, a genetic abnormality that was generally passed through the father. It was then that we abruptly halted our quest to have a child.

I had no idea if Samantha knew this. Actually I doubted it. When her mother told her to get in touch with Peter should she need help, I can't imagine she would have told her the man she thought was her father was not. She had endured enough sadness already. Perhaps her mother thought when Peter met Samantha, he would realize the connection because of her appearance and help her. I'm sure subconsciously that had been my motivation although I was unwilling to admit the truth to myself. Now I was bound to her in ways I wasn't before.

And the most agonizing question was did Peter know about his daughter? I couldn't believe my wonderful husband would have abandoned his own child, not as much as he had wanted children. But if our marriage had been at stake, would he have decided he could never admit his infidelity? When I went through his finances after he died in settling the estate, there was no sign that he had ever sent money to an unknown woman. But that is not to say he couldn't have disguised support payments in some way. I would never know for sure what Peter had done.

"You're sure the quiet one. Don't you want to know more about it?" Jay said.

"I guess so." I was looking out the side window so he couldn't see how upset I was. I wanted to drop the subject, but that would make Jay wonder why. And knowledge is power, they say. So the more I knew, the better I could help Samantha.

"Well, all the physical things like the eyes and the ears and the sunken chest are part of it. I guess as babies there can be considerable difficulty with feeding, and some need to be fed by tube for a while. Their speech development is delayed, and some are diagnosed with an autistic spectrum disorder. A number of them show signs of clumsiness, stubbornness, and irritability."

127

"Well, that last sounds like ninety percent of the population," I said trying for a light tone. I couldn't bear to share my revelation with Jay at this time. I had to process it for myself before I could tell anyone else.

Jay went on. "About a tenth of children with the syndrome have developmental disabilities and need special education. Do you think she falls into that category?"

"No. Not at all. I think she has at least average intelligence. Apparently she's had a hard row to hoe with being taunted and harassed. Given half a chance, I think she'll do all right for herself." I was trying to reassure myself as much as anything. What if she couldn't support herself? What would I do?

"Well, you're a remarkable woman, Liz. I think you've earned a star in heaven."

I couldn't stand the thought that he was under the illusion I was selfless and noble. I knew now, though I wouldn't admit it to myself, I had realized all along that Samantha was no doubt Peter's love child. And if that were true, was there something I had done to drive Peter into another woman's arms? I didn't feel heroic; I felt guilty.

We arrived at my house just as the heavens opened up and a deluge ensued. Of course I hadn't taken an umbrella.

"You're going to get soaked," Jay warned.

"I'll run. I'm just glad it held off till now. It's been a wonderful weekend, Jay."

He pulled me to him and kissed me hard. "I haven't been so happy since my wife died. Thanks for bringing some sunshine to my life."

I pointed out the window, "Sunshine?"

"Hey, when you're around it feels like a sunny day even when it's pouring."

I laughed. He was so sweet. "I guess I'll see you Thursday

evening then."

"I wish I could take you to dinner beforehand, but I've got a meeting. But let's go for a drink afterward."

"It's a date."

I grabbed my bag that I'd stashed behind the seat, jumped out of the truck, and raced to the porch. Once under cover, I turned and waved goodbye.

Jay threw me a kiss, backed out of the driveway, and drove away.

I stood on the porch for several minutes, emotions swirling through me like the wind that was whipping the trees into a frenzy in the yard. The weekend had been so lovely. Though my life was comfortable enough, it was bland and predictable. Jay had brought excitement and surprise that lifted it out of the ordinary. I knew that being with him would enrich me immeasurably.

But now that I realized the truth about Samantha, how would that affect our relationship? I felt more than ever now that I owed her a chance at a decent life. And I wasn't sure it was possible without my help. I had to assist her at least until she could stand on her own feet.

I knew that sooner or later I would have to tell Jay the truth or he would begin to wonder why I felt such a responsibility. Even though he'd lauded my efforts, helping Samantha could interfere in our relationship and he might begin to resent her. Maybe he was way too big hearted to feel that way, but I couldn't be sure.

Finally I was able to pull myself together and go in the house. Samantha was in the living room reading a book from my bookshelf.

"Hello," she said. "Did you have a nice trip?" She actually smiled a little.

"Yes, thank you. And what have you been doing?"

"Lots of reading. You have so many good books."

"Well, help yourself. They're just sitting there waiting to be read."

I went into my bedroom and unpacked and put a load in the washing machine. Then I went back into the living room and sat down opposite Samantha.

I sat there for a moment while she read. Finally she realized I was looking at her. "You want something?"

"I do. I feel if we're going to live together we should know something about each other. Can you tell me a little about yourself?"

She shrugged. "Not much to tell." She laid the book down on the sofa cushion beside her and clasped her hands together in her lap. She seemed a bit defensive, as if I was going to interrogate her unmercifully.

"Have you always lived in Wilmington?"

"All my life. But my folks moved from Greensboro before I was born."

"How old are you, Samantha?"

"Twenty."

I glanced down at my lap as I mentally added and subtracted the years. That would have been about the time that I was well into the throes of trying to get pregnant. We were trying in vitro fertilization, and it was a pretty harrowing time, waiting every month to see if it had taken. It not only was costing us thousands of dollars, but it was putting a strain on our relationship, especially our sex life. And it would have been just before we learned that Peter could be carrying the defective gene. I'm sure he would never have taken a chance with any partner had he been aware of that.

I know it had been a particularly difficult time for both of us, but I never realized how emotionally fragile Peter must have been. As devastated as I was to learn of his probable infidelity, under the circumstances I knew I should forgive him. What good would it do either Samantha or me to carry around bitterness over something that happened so many years before? Still, I had to deal with the result of his unfaithfulness, and I wasn't sure I could do that with grace. Perhaps I wasn't quite as forgiving as I hoped I would be.

"Just out of curiosity, what was your mother's maiden name?" I asked.

She looked at me like she wanted to ask *why do you care?* But she said instead, "Sanderson. Ella Sanderson."

I managed to hesitate no more than a few seconds to reply although my heart felt as though it had stopped. I quickly said, "I thought I might have known her before she was married but apparently not." That wasn't quite the truth but close enough.

I remembered Peter speaking fondly of Ella Sanderson, one of his customers, who at the time was single. And then one day I realized he hadn't mentioned her name in quite a while, and I asked him what had happened to her. He told me she'd gotten married and moved away.

"Tell me about your family, Samantha." I don't know why I persisted in questioning her like this. It was a masochistic thing to do, but I couldn't contain my curiosity.

"Mom worked in a bookstore and Dad sold real estate. But he was sick for many years, so we struggled financially. I was an only child. I hardly ever saw any of my grandparents because they lived so far away. They're all dead now." She looked down at her lap with a sad expression and picked at the cording on a sofa cushion. There was no doubt she was alone in the world. It must be difficult not to have any living relatives. At least I had a sister even though she lived out west.

"Did you like Wilmington?" I decided to throw in an innocuous question so she didn't think I was prying about her family.

She smiled slightly, which seemed the most she was capable

of. "I loved the beach. That was my favorite place in the world." Her smile faded. "But I hated school. I really didn't have any friends."

I had one last question even though I'd asked her before why she'd come to my door asking for my husband. Would she tell me a different story this time? "Do you know why your mother told you to look up Peter?" Would Samantha confess she knew he was her father?

She shook her head. "I don't know. I guess they were friends or something. She'd never mentioned his name before that."

I felt great relief. If she knew who Peter really was, she could make demands on me and I didn't want to be in the position of knowing I *had* to help her. For the time being I was willing to do what I could. But I knew I wasn't going to tell her the truth, at least not now.

"It's your turn," Samantha said.

I'd forgotten it was a two-way street. "Uh . . . well, I was married for thirty-four years. Worked in a jewelry store. Nothing exciting."

"Do you have kids?"

"No I don't. I wasn't able to get pregnant." I didn't know why I added the last. It wasn't as if I owed her that bit of information.

She looked at me with sympathy. "That's too bad. Mom used to always tell me I was the best thing that ever happened to her."

I felt a twinge of jealousy along with a surge of relief that her mother had cherished her. It would have been unbearably sad to know that Peter's child had never been loved. "I'm sure you were," I said.

# Chapter Eighteen

Monday morning Samantha left for work. I could tell from her silence at breakfast how much she dreaded it. As much as I felt like saying, "Just forget it. Stay here and I'll support you," I knew that wouldn't work for either of us. I truly wanted to be alone, especially since Jay had come into my life, so I had no intention of taking on Samantha as a lifelong commitment. And I wouldn't be doing her any favor either to make her dependent on me forever. She had to gain the skills that would enable her to support herself for the rest of her life. Somehow, together we had to make that happen.

I went to my studio hoping to submerge myself in my painting, an excuse to postpone trying to figure out where my life was going. If I'd had only one thing to worry about I probably could have handled it. But two—Jay and Samantha—was putting my capacity to handle anxiety into overload.

I decided that it might be therapeutic to take a canvas and, instead of trying to paint my usual safe and conservative still life, start flinging colors at it with abandon. It might serve me better than a good hard cry. I squeezed generous dabs of every hue of the rainbow onto my palette and started swiping on wide swathes in every direction. I began to develop a rhythm: slash, slash, dip into paint, splatter. A momentum built up until I was almost frenetically adding more and more layers of paint. It looked like a mess, but it was helping release all the pent up emotion that had been building in me.

My canvas was a celebration of my neuroses in an orgy of splattered paint when a knock came at my door. I considered pretending I wasn't there. A second knock made me lay down my brush and open the door. It was Rachel. She looked at me, then looked at my picture and her eyes opened wide.

"Are you okay? Or is this some new style you're trying out?"

I couldn't help but laugh. It felt good. "Just getting some things off my chest."

"Do you want to talk about it?"

I considered it a moment. "Yeah, I guess so."

"Why don't we go to lunch then?"

Since the weather had changed from rainy and cool the day before to sunny and almost spring-like, we decided to brave the patio at Café Europa which had tall heaters around the perimeter emitting enough heat to ward off any chill.

"So is it Jay or is it Samantha?" Rachel asked after we'd ordered.

"You don't beat around the bush much, do you?" Rachel always read me like a book.

"What else could it be?" She threw up her hands.

I tried to look innocent, but I knew it wasn't working. "My washing machine broke down. I've overdrawn my bank account."

She grinned. "Possibly, but I don't think so. You had that 'Jay' look in your eye."

"Am I that transparent?"

She merely smiled and took a sip of the wine she'd ordered. Then she got serious. "I hope he hasn't dumped you."

I toyed with my silverware while deciding whether to confide in her or not. Peter had always been my sounding board, and I sorely missed having someone to talk things over with. Meredith had such a jaundiced view of life I didn't want that to taint my relationship with Jay. Rachel had always been sympathetic and supportive.

"It's both. I spent the weekend with Jay."

Rachel's eyes widened. "Wow! I hope it turned out well. Or were you trying to metaphorically paint him out of your life back there?"

I shook my head. "Oh, no. Definitely not. But between his son and his problems and Samantha living with me, it's going to be virtually impossible to spend much time together. Quality time that is."

She got a devilish look in her eye. "Hmmm. Could you clarify 'quality time'?"

"Use your imagination, girl," I said, grinning. "But I don't think we're going to spend many weekends together. Brian was at his grandparents. But that doesn't happen often."

She chewed on her lip. "I see what you mean. You do have a conundrum."

We both sat in silence for a few minutes.

Finally she said, "I think what you're doing for Samantha is selfless of you, Liz, but if it's going to mess up your personal life, don't you think you could make other arrangements for her?"

I shrugged. "Like what?"

"Well, it would be hard, but maybe tell her you're sorry and just can't have her there after all. Surely there are agencies in town that can help her out some way."

The waiter brought our salads, and we both ate for a while without speaking. It was a comfortable silence. Finally I said, "Rachel, I'm going to tell you something that not another soul knows. And I'm swearing you to secrecy. I don't want this to come out."

She looked at me in alarm. "What on earth?"

"Samantha is my husband's child. I only just figured it out."

135

Her mouth dropped open. "Are you sure? How do you know?"

"When I was unable to get pregnant, we had genetic testing done. It showed Peter carried a gene for something called Noonan Syndrome and that's why we stopped trying in vitro fertilization. It just couldn't be a fluke that Samantha's mother told her to contact Peter and she happens to have all the exact characteristics of the syndrome. I wouldn't have known all this, but Jay was curious about her appearance and looked it up on line."

"You're sure of this just because of her looks?"

"That isn't all. I asked Samantha what her mother's maiden name was, and it turned out she was Peter's client about twenty years ago when she was single. I couldn't bring myself to tell Jay the implications of his discovery."

All she could say was, "Oh, my god!"

"I don't think I'll tell her. She has enough problems in her life. Why add the fact the man she thought was her father was not related to her?"

"I think I'll have another glass of wine," Rachel said as she waved to the waiter at the far end of the patio. "I need reinforcements."

We both ordered refills and sat sipping from our goblets, both of us deep in concentration.

Finally Rachel spoke. "Just to play devil's advocate here, why should you have to pay so dearly for a mistake your husband made so many years ago? To put it plainly, he cheated on you, and now you get to deal with the results. That seems really unfair to me."

I thought about that for a while. "You have a point. Jay has to deal with Brian's problems because he's Brian's dad, and that's what you do for your children. But Samantha really isn't my responsibility. She's an adult, and I'm not related to her."

Rachel just looked at me without comment.

"I need to think about what I do next. Let's change the subject," I said. "What's happening with your writing these days? It seems we're always talking about me."

"I've sold two more short stories, one to a literary magazine, and one to an anthology. At this rate I may even have to get a computer." Once she began talking about her writing she was all smiles. After all the disappointments and rejections she'd had, it seemed that her career had finally taken off.

"That's fantastic, Rachel! I'm so proud of you."

We went on to talk about the tenants of Sternberger Center and the subject of Samantha never came up again.

Back in my studio I thought about our conversation. Should I think about my own welfare first? Jay seemed to me at this point like one in a million. I was not a young woman. How many chances would I have for a loving relationship for the rest of my life? If we got serious, although I knew it premature to be considering this, I would have to tell Jay the truth about Samantha. He already had the onerous job of keeping Brian on the straight and narrow. If we were to become a couple, would he want to have partial responsibility for a woman who was my husband's love child? That seemed like too much to ask of him. I was wondering if it was too much to ask of myself.

By the time I was ready to go home, I'd decided to tell Samantha that I'd start searching for someone who was looking for a roommate to help pay the rent or the mortgage. Since the economic downturn, many people were taking boarders into their homes or apartments to make ends meet. If Samantha couldn't pay the entire rent, I'd even subsidize her in order to find her a place of her own.

When I walked in the door, I could see the red light flashing on my answering machine. I played back the message.

"Ms. Raynor. This is Isabel Jenkins calling from Fairview Assisted Living. It's about Samantha. She slipped on a wet spot in the kitchen and fell at about three o'clock. We called an ambulance, and they took her to Wesley Long Hospital. She asked me to call you."

Not a word about how badly she was injured. At first I was going to call Fairview to see what they could tell me but decided it made much more sense to go to the hospital and find out for myself. I was so upset I couldn't find my car keys for several minutes though they were right where I'd left them, and then I was halfway out the door before I remembered my purse. I couldn't begin to understand what the implications of this would mean and the very thought made me ill.

I drove above the speed limit down Wendover Avenue to the hospital where I had to park in Outer Mongolia. I rushed into the emergency room and, when I gave Samantha's name, was ushered into a cubicle in the back. Samantha, paler than usual, lay on the bed with her eyes closed, an IV attached to her arm. Her left leg was in an inflatable splint.

"Samantha?" I said in a low voice. I didn't want to wake her if she was asleep.

She opened her eyes and grimaced in pain. "Hi," she said in a weak voice.

"What happened?" I asked.

She spoke slowly, obviously in pain. "Somebody dropped a tray on the floor, and I stepped in the food and slipped. I broke my leg real bad."

"Oh, Samantha. I'm so sorry." I slipped my hand over hers and squeezed it. It seemed as if the whole world was aligned against her. How much more bad luck could she endure?

The doctor came into the cubicle carrying a clipboard. "I'm Samantha's friend, and she lives with me," I explained. "She has no relatives. Can you tell me about her injury?"

"Samantha?" he asked. "Is that all right?"

She nodded.

"She has a bad break of the thigh bone. I'm going to have to insert a rod. We're planning surgery for tomorrow morning."

"What's the prognosis, doctor?"

"She'll have to have extensive therapy, but hopefully she'll eventually be able to walk normally."

I could hardly believe what I was hearing. I felt terrible for her but sorry for myself as well. So much for my plans for finding her another place to live. It looked like I was going to have Samantha around for quite a while.

# CHAPTER NINETEEN

Samantha's surgery lasted several hours the following morning. The surgeon came out afterward and told me it had gone as well as could be expected as far as fixing the leg, but Samantha had some trouble with blood pressure so they were keeping her in the hospital a little longer than usual to monitor it. I stayed by her side for a while after she got back to her room, but she was in a lot of pain and the nurses kept her on medication that caused her to sleep most of the time.

She was in the hospital for another six days. Whatever problems had arisen with her blood pressure seemed to have been resolved without medication. At first I was worried about how the bills were going to be paid, but I learned that Fairview's liability insurance would cover the cost. That was the one small ray of sunshine in the whole unhappy episode.

I continued to go to my studio in the mornings and visited her for a while every afternoon.

On Wednesday morning, Rachel came into my studio shortly after I arrived.

"Have you given any more thought to what you're going to do about Samantha?" she asked.

"The whole situation has changed. And not for the better." I gestured to the desk chair for her to sit. I perched on the edge of the desk, though I would have preferred to lie down on the floor and bawl like a baby. Maybe if we could have tantrums as adults we'd feel better in times of stress.

"Good lord, Liz. What happened?"

"She slipped on some food at work and broke her thigh. She's going to be laid up for a long time and will need weeks of therapy."

Rachel cried, "Oh, no!" shaking her head in sympathy. She patted my knee. "You've gotten through worse things; you'll get through this. You're strong, Liz. And you know what? This could be a test for Jay as well. If he'll stick by you now, you'll know he's serious about you. And that's what you want, don't you?"

I wanted to cry, but I held it in. "Well, sure. But I didn't imagine having to test him like this. Maybe he *is* special, but with the loss of his wife and now his son's problems, maybe this added complication is more than even a saint would want to deal with. I don't mean to sound ugly, but I feel as if I have an albatross around my neck."

"From what little I've been around him, I think he can cope. But all you can do is see how it all plays out and think positive."

"You know what? I'm sick of having to think positive. Some days I'd like to wallow in my misery." I tried for a smile and managed a weak one.

Rachel stood up. "I know how to cure that. Let's go to the Cold Stone Creamery at noon and get one of their decadent sundaes."

"I've never had one." I blew my nose. "You think that will work?"

"You've never tried one? Oh my god, they are so rich you won't want to eat again for a week. There's one with chocolate ice cream, chocolate chips, brownies, and fudge sauce. If that doesn't release endorphins, I don't know what would."

I couldn't help but laugh. "That sounds better than getting drunk. Let's do it."

And so at noon we drove to Friendly Shopping Center on the other side of town to gorge ourselves on an orgy of calories. I'm

141

not sure the bloated feeling afterward was any better than a hangover would be, but the fact we steered clear of all serious matters and chatted about frivolous things raised my spirits. We had taken separate cars so Rachel could return to Sternberger and I could visit Samantha.

She was more alert than she'd been the day before, but I could tell she was in a lot of pain. She tried to be brave.

"So, how are you feeling?" I asked.

She shrugged which made her wince. "Hangin' in there." If she was "hanging in there," it was barely by the tips of her fingers.

Samantha had never been easy to talk to but it was harder than ever now. She was stoic and close-mouthed. At least she didn't bemoan her fate. I thought of the woman in the Fairview home who couldn't stop complaining. Samantha would never be like that.

I had brought a small bunch of flowers that I bought at the Harris Teeter grocery store and arranged them in a dollar vase that I'd picked up somewhere for such an occasion. She watched me silently.

"I thought these might cheer you up," I said.

"Thanks," she said without enthusiasm.

I stayed a little while longer, trying every now and then to start a conversation only to be met with one-syllable answers. Finally I said, "I can tell you're tired, so I'll go along and let you rest."

This proved to be the pattern for the rest of her stay in the hospital. There were days when I wondered why I bothered to go.

On Wednesday Rachel and I served breakfast at Urban Ministry as usual. There were more new faces than ever before.

"Do you think the economy is ever going to turn around?"

142

Rachel asked as we dished up food side by side. "The homeless rate is getting higher and higher."

"I know. But the sad thing is that often when they can get a job, like Samantha, they don't make enough money to afford a decent apartment. It's a mess."

"Thank god you came to her rescue. I'm assuming that under the circumstances you've decided to keep things as they are at least for now."

"I have to, Rachel. I don't have a choice."

"Well, that's not true. You could turn her over to social services or something. But, then, you're a saint."

"Hardly." I didn't feel the least bit saintly. In fact, guilt over my resentment of the circumstances that put me in this position gnawed at my insides all the time.

On Thursday night when I got to class, several other students were already there so I couldn't say much to Jay. He came by as I was setting up my easel and said softly, "Coffee afterward?"

Of course I said yes.

The model that evening was a young woman about Samantha's age. She was strikingly attractive with long blond hair, blue eyes, anda body that was perfection. I couldn't help but think how unfair it was for some to be so blessed with physical loveliness, while others were cursed from birth with features that didn't conform to the standards we set for beauty. Not that Samantha's features were monstrous, not at all. But just far enough off the mark to make her the brunt of cruel remarks and teasing. And having to endure such taunting can leave indelible wounds in one's psyche. I wondered what sort of person she would have been had she looked more like everyone else.

When class was over, Jay and I went downstairs to Café Europa.

As we sat at a table waiting for our coffee, he took my hand.

"So how are you? I've been thinking a lot about our weekend. That was really special, Liz, We need to do that again. Soon."

My heart did a little tap dance. "I'd love that. I might have a problem, though."

He frowned. "Why is that?"

I sighed. "Samantha slipped in the kitchen where she worked and broke her leg. It's bad, Jay. It's her thigh bone. The doctors did surgery and put a rod in it."

"Oh no, Liz. That's terrible. Where is she?"

"At Wesley Long. She'll probably be there till the first of the week. Then I guess she'll be at my house."

"Jesus. I imagine that will be a long recovery period."

"Yes, she'll need lots of therapy. And I guess I'm the designated driver. I don't know how else she'd get there."

He looked at me with deep concern in his eyes. "Liz, you're an angel. But you don't have to do all this you know."

I concentrated on stirring cream into my coffee, anything to keep from having to look him in the eye.

"I'm afraid I do, Jay. I can't explain it to you now, but I *have* to do it."

He rubbed his forehead as though a severe headache had struck. "Between Brian and Samantha we've got ourselves in a pickle, don't we?"

"It doesn't mean we can't see each other, does it?"

"Well, no, but it's a little hard to have intimate weekends when we can't go to either house."

"Tell you what. Samantha will still be in the hospital this weekend. Could you get away for a bit to come to my house?" I watched him looking thoughtfully into his cup as he groped for the right answer.

"Right now I don't think I should spend the night. Brian seems to be doing well, but I don't feel I can trust him not to have a party if I'm gone. Let's do something Saturday afternoon.

Then I can let him know I'll be home at a reasonable hour so he won't think he can get away with anything."

Good lord, I thought. What a way to carry on a romance. It seemed like we were destined to have a relationship that became more complicated at every turn.

"What do you have in mind?" I asked. I think I was afraid he was going to say let's spend the day in your bedroom while we have the chance. If he had, I would have wondered what he saw in me: an easy lay? A desperate woman? A way to satisfy his libido?

"There's a new exhibit at Reynolda House that I've been anxious to see," he said. "It's a show of American impressionists on loan from the National Academy Museum. They have some work by Childe Hassam, William Merritt Chase, and John Singer Sargent. Would you be interested in going there?"

Reynolda House is the former home of the founder of a tobacco company in Winston-Salem, about thirty miles west of Greensboro. Not only has the beautiful home been preserved the way it was when the family lived there, but an added art gallery features outstanding exhibits.

"I'd love it," I said, feeling a sense of relief. Why couldn't I trust my instincts about Jay?

He walked me to the parking garage where we both had parked and made sure I was safely in my car. Before I got in the driver's seat, he leaned over and gave me a lingering kiss. "How about I pick you up around eleven on Saturday? Then we can get something to eat in Winston-Salem before we go on to the gallery."

"I'll visit Samantha early so I'll be back home by then."

I hummed "Getting to Know You" as I drove home. At my age the familiar tunes from my youth always held sway over the current music. I knew all the lyrics from *The King and I* but would be hard pressed to hum the songs popular now other than a few country ballads.

# CHAPTER TWENTY

I awoke the next morning to see the yard and shrubs covered with a light layer of snow. Spring in Greensboro is always a chameleon. One day it will be sunny and warm, and the next it can revert to winter. You never knew what to expect nor did the weathermen. They were often as surprised as everyone else.

I went to the living room window and looked out at the street. Apparently the pavement had been warm enough to melt what little snow had fallen, and it seemed to be clear.

I ate a hurried breakfast and drove to the hospital so I could get back by eleven. Samantha seemed even more alert this morning.

"Aren't you kind of early?" she asked.

"I have plans for this afternoon," I said without elaborating.

"The doctor thinks I can probably go home on Tuesday," she said.

*Home*, I thought. She's already decided that my house is her house. Or maybe it was just a figure of speech. Besides, since Peter was her father I guess it is her home as much as it is mine.

"That's good," I said, even though I dreaded what it meant: the necessity of waiting on her, the trips she'd have to make to therapy and to doctors. I'd always yearned for a child. Now that Samantha had come into my life, I realized how much of an impact and a disruption it brings. I was sure that if she had been my own flesh and blood, I wouldn't have felt it was a burden. Or at least I hoped I wouldn't. No one knows what kind of a mother she might be until she's faced with the reality of it.

Our visit was interrupted several times by nurses taking vitals, therapists stopping in, all the sundry personnel making their rounds in the mornings, so I finally told her I had to leave.

Jay pulled into the driveway at exactly eleven o'clock.

"I thought we'd eat at the Village Tavern," he said as he headed toward I-40 and Winston-Salem.

Reynolda Village, where the restaurant is located, is a charming assortment of shops and restaurants in what had once been the outbuildings on the Reynolda estate.

We talked about our favorite painters who would be featured in the show as we drove toward Winston. Jay was a fan of Hassam, while I had fallen in love with John Singer Sargent. Peter and I had once flown to Boston to see a Sargent exhibit at the Boston Museum of Art. The actual paintings are so much more powerful than reproductions in books and magazines. I'd been blown away by his gorgeous larger-than-life portraits and his watercolor landscapes.

At the Village Tavern I ordered a Chinese chicken salad and Jay had Chicken Colorado, a delicious looking entrée that included bacon, barbeque sauce, cheese, black beans and rice. And probably contained three thousand calories. But slender Jay didn't have to worry about his waistline. How I envied him that.

We toured Reynolda House prior to going to the attached gallery. A long rectangular white house with green roof and trim built in 1917, its façade features large windows allowing a grand view into the formal gardens which cover four acres. The reception hall is the most spectacular room in the house, a huge room with dual staircases flanking a large fireplace and a second floor balcony on all four sides. It served as the heart of the home where the Reynoldses entertained. A paneled study and a library featuring sofas and chairs upholstered in a riot of flowers opened off this central space.

The sleek modern art gallery which had been added onto the house is as austere as the house is cheerful and homey. But the beautiful exhibit warmed up its ascetic formality with the lush colors and glorious landscapes. Jay and I took our time admiring each painting.

"I never thought of Sargent as an impressionist," I said to Jay. I'd never had an art history course, and my knowledge of art and artists is sketchy and limited.

"The British considered him one, but the French didn't," he said. "He knew many of the European Impressionists because he lived there. In fact his painting, 'Claude Monet Painting at the Edge of the Wood' was done in that style."

We spent most of the afternoon in the gallery. Finally, reluctant to leave, we headed back to Greensboro.

"Where do you want to go to dinner?" Jay asked when we were on the highway toward home.

"Are you willing to try my cooking? I'm not much in the kitchen, but I can put together an omelet or salad or something else that's simple."

"That sounds fine. That lunch I ate was enough for three meals, so I'm not very hungry at all."

I felt turn-about was fair play. He'd cooked for me at his house; I should do the same for him. Though, admittedly, my culinary skills left much to be desired.

We decided that tomato soup and toasted cheese sandwiches sounded good to both of us. Jay put the sandwiches together while I opened a can of soup and added milk. We stood side by side as he grilled the sandwiches over one burner and I stirred the soup on the next. He reached for my hand and held it as he wielded the spatula with his left one. And so we stood holding hands like teenagers while we tended dinner. Once we settled at the dining table it seemed so domestic and *right*. I looked in Jay's eyes across the table, and he winked at me.

Afterward we sat on the sofa together. We began by discussing the art show, but soon Jay had pulled me to him and kissed me long and hard. He held me close for quite a while without saying a word. Finally he sat back and said, "I know it's going to be complicated, Liz, but I want to keep seeing you, no matter how difficult it is. These obstacles aren't going to be around forever. We can't let them keep us apart."

"Let's put a name to it—Brian and Samantha. Not just inanimate 'obstacles' that we can overcome. They are living, breathing people who have their own problems."

"Yes, you're right. That was a poor choice of words. What I meant was they're going to grow up and get a life of their own."

"We hope."

"Brian's almost seventeen. In another year he'll be old enough to join the army."

"The army? Good god, Jay, I hope not. Surely you don't want him to do that."

"He says that's what he wants to do. Maybe he'll get the discipline he needs. I support him fully in whatever he wants to do, as long as it's not illegal."

"I just hope he thinks it through. I'd hate to see a son go off to Afghanistan."

"He knows how anti-war I am. Maybe that's what's pushing him to do it. Stick it to the old man."

"That's a hell of a reason. Get yourself blown to bits to get back at your father."

Jay shook his head. "It's ironic. It was the opposite with me and my father. He was a career army guy, and he wanted me to follow in his footsteps. He thought following a career in art was for pansies, quote, unquote. Maybe his genes are coming through in his grandson."

"Oh, Jay," I said. "How sad. Is he still alive?"

"Yeah. That's the grandfather Brian was visiting last weekend. That's probably where he got the idea to enlist."

"Maybe he'll change his mind in the next year."

"Not on account of me. I know the more I say about it, the more the idea will become entrenched in his mind. So I'm keeping my mouth shut."

"And then there's Samantha," I said.

"Yeah, there's that."

If we were putting our cards on the table, I knew it was my turn to uncover my hand. I wanted to continue my involvement with Jay, but to do so, I had to be honest with him.

"Remember on the drive home from your place last weekend you told me you'd discovered what was wrong with her?"

"Sure. I said she had Noonan Syndrome. Never heard of it before, but that's the genius of the Internet."

"The minute you said that, everything changed for me."

He gave me a puzzled look. "Why on earth?"

"When Peter and I were trying to have a child we went through all kinds of medical procedures and tests. Finally they did a genetic study, and they found out that Peter carried the gene for Noonan Syndrome. That's when we stopped trying."

Jay opened his mouth to say something and closed it again. He looked at me sadly before gathering me in his arms again.

"That must have been a shock," he said in my ear. "How did you make the connection with her?"

I pulled away from him, but I knew that tears were close to brimming over now. "She came to my door about nine or ten months ago asking for Peter. When I told her he was dead, she broke down crying. She'd come all the way from Wilmington to see him, but she told me little else except that her mother, who had recently died, had told her to look for Peter Raynor."

"Did you realize then who she was?"

"No, I think deep down in my subconscious I was pretty sure, but I wouldn't let myself think about it. She didn't have any place to go, so I took her to that motel up on Summit. I didn't see her again for six months when I spotted her at Urban Ministry where I was helping serve breakfast."

"She was homeless by then I guess."

"Yes, she lived on the street for a short while before going to the shelter. Even though I wouldn't admit to myself exactly who she was, I felt compelled to help her. A friend lined up the job at the assisted living place, but I found she wouldn't make enough money to rent anywhere. That's when I decided to take her in."

"And then I told you about Noonan Syndrome."

The tears finally released themselves and began to spill down my cheeks. "I couldn't be in denial any longer, Jay. I knew she was Peter's daughter. It was confirmed for me when I asked her what her mother's maiden name was. She'd been one of Peter's customers when she was single."

"Do you think she knows?"

"No, I don't. I believe her mother kept it a secret, but when she was dying told her to look up Peter. She probably felt Peter would immediately realize who she was and help her."

"Oh, Liz," Jay said. He reached in his pocket and pulled out a hankie and handed it to me.

I wiped my eyes and blew my nose and tried to regain my composure. "I just have to help her, Jay. I don't know how long it will last. I had hopes she could go to GTCC and learn some job skills. But now with this leg. . . ."

"Look," he said taking both my hands in his, "this can't last forever. It might take longer than my dealing with Brian. But as soon as she's able, I think the community college would be the right thing to do. If there's any way I can help—transportation,

152

whatever, I'll be glad to."

I don't know why I had any doubts about how Jay would react when I told him the truth about Samantha. His compassion only made me love him more.

I stood up. "You don't have to go home for a little while yet, do you?"

"Did you have a game of cards in mind?" he asked with a wry smile.

"Maybe a round of hearts?" I said, taking his hand and leading him to the bedroom.

# Chapter Twenty-One

Samantha was released from the hospital the following Tuesday. She used a walker to get around which was a slow and painful process. My house was not designed for an invalid, and she ended up navigating the steps up to the front porch by sitting on them and hoisting herself up backward one step at a time. Thankfully the weather had warmed up, and the snow had all melted. Still, it was very awkward helping her to her feet once she'd reached the porch. I knew it was going to be difficult to help her in and out of the house. My back wouldn't last very long even though she was small.

We settled into a routine. I'd fix breakfast for both of us, then I would go off to Sternberger and she would go back to bed or lie on the sofa and watch TV. I'd come home for lunch, and three afternoons a week I took her to therapy. Luckily the therapist was on our side of town so it was a short drive. Because it was close, I could drop her off, and then run errands or clean house before picking her up again.

I kept my routine, serving breakfast at Urban Ministry on Wednesday mornings and going to art class on Thursday nights. Jay wanted to go somewhere the first weekend Samantha was home, but I told him I was simply too exhausted and she took up too much of my time to try to get away just yet.

"I hope you don't kill yourself over this, Liz," he said looking stern.

"I won't, I promise," I said. "It's bound to get better soon."

"Can I take her to her therapy some days?"

"I'm afraid it's when you have your afternoon classes. But thanks for asking. I hope you understand, Jay. I'd rather go out with you than anything else I can think of, but it'll just have to wait for now."

"You understood when I put you off in my concern over Brian. I guess I can be as patient as you were."

I looked at him with longing. "Do you think we're destined to be kept apart? It's beginning to feel like it."

It was after class, but several of the students were still putting away their materials on the other side of the room. So Jay simply took my hands and squeezed them. "No, Liz, I think we're destined to be together. We'll work through this."

I just squeezed his hands back.

The next day I got a call from Meredith. I realized I hadn't talked to her in a while, but I'd been too busy to think about her.

"Long time no hear. Are you avoiding me, Liz?"

"Of course not. It's just that I've been snowed under."

"How can that be? You don't work. All you do is fool around with your painting."

I resented that. And I didn't like her tone of condescension. She knew nothing about what I was going through. I felt like hanging up on her, but I didn't.

"Samantha broke her leg at work. I have to take her to therapy several times a week."

"Jeez Louise, Liz, I knew that arrangement wasn't going to work out. Can't you find some social service that will take care of her? This is ridiculous."

I was seething. Meredith's attitude had been getting to me for some time now. It was turning into a toxic relationship, and I didn't need it. "I'm sorry, Meredith, but I'm just too busy to talk to you now." And I hung up. It felt good.

On the other hand, Rachel had been offering to take Samantha to therapy some of the time. I'd turned her down because I felt it was my responsibility and I didn't want to put the burden on anyone else. But finally by the third week, I relented.

Rachel had come into my studio and asked how things were going.

"It's been tough," I admitted. "It's so hard to get Samantha in and out of the house."

"You look exhausted, Liz," she said. "Please let me help you out. How about this: on Wednesdays after we serve breakfast at Urban Ministry, why don't we go out to lunch and I can take her to therapy that afternoon."

"I've been going home for lunch so I can fix her something. I'll take you up on that if you'll come eat with us first."

"It's a deal."

The following Wednesday we went to my house following our stint at the shelter. Samantha was in the living room watching TV when we arrived.

"Hello, Samantha," Rachel said as she went over and sat beside her. "Remember me? I serve breakfast at the Urban Ministry with Liz, and I met you there a while back."

Samantha studied her face. "Oh, yeah. I remember you."

"Well. I'm going to take you to therapy this afternoon. In fact I'll be doing it every Wednesday."

"Okay." And she turned back to her program.

I looked at Rachel and grimaced at Samantha's lack of social skills, but she smiled at me and winked. I marveled at her ability to take things in stride. She had a certain grace about her that I admired and envied.

As Rachel and I fixed soup and sandwiches for lunch, she went on about my house since it was the first time she'd been there.

"This place is charming," she raved. "Did you do the work or had it been renovated when you bought it?"

"Peter and I did a lot of it, and when we couldn't do something like electrical work, we hired people. We spent many years getting it to this point."

"Well, you should be very proud of it."

"I am."

During lunch Rachel and I carried on most of the conversation. Samantha was her usual reticent self even though Rachel tried hard to include her.

When they left to go to the therapist, Rachel took my hand and whispered, "Hang in there," as Samantha bumped her way down the front steps on her bottom. It was an inglorious way to get in and out of the house, but I couldn't see undertaking the expense of a ramp when I knew she'd be able to do steps in a few weeks.

I felt liberated if only for a few hours. The weather had turned spring-like, and I decided to go to the Bicentennial Gardens for a walk. The earliest of the blooming trees had burst forth in a haze of white and pink, and the tulips and daffodils were about to fade away in favor of the multi-colored azaleas. A walk along the winding trails boosted my spirits and helped me put my circumstances in perspective. I thought about Samantha's mother having to deal with all the harassment her daughter faced in growing up. It must have torn her heart out to have her daughter come home in tears time after time. Things were bound to improve once Samantha was able to navigate on her own again. When I got home, Rachel and Samantha had not yet returned. Rachel had mentioned something about taking her out for a sundae after therapy. I felt she was trying to give me some additional time alone, and I appreciated it.

The telephone rang, and it was someone from the bank calling. I'd had an account at the same bank all my married life, and I knew the manager personally.

"Mrs. Raynor, this is Margaret Sutliff," the caller said. Only once before had the manager called me and that was when Peter died and she called to offer her condolences.

"Well, hi Margaret," I said. "What's up?"

"I think we have a problem," she said, her voice sounding troubled. "Your mortgage check has bounced along with some others."

"What? I don't understand. The money is supposed to be deposited automatically the first of every month from my investment account."

"Well, this time it wasn't. I think you need to check with your broker and find out what's going on."

As soon as I hung up, I dialed Ron Pemberton's number. I wasn't at all prepared for what the voice said on the other end. The number had been disconnected.

# CHAPTER TWENTY-TWO

Bile rose in my throat as I thought about the possibilities. Something definitely was all wrong. I barely knew Ron Pemberton. Peter had known him for years as fellow financial advisors, and when Peter got sick and knew his chances of survival were slim, he asked Ron to take over his customers. He didn't want any interruption in their service.

I'd never worried about my investments. Peter had handled them all our married lives, and after he died I just assumed my assets were in good hands. With the economic downturn, I could see that my bottom line was being affected just like everyone else's. It was alarming, but I knew that someday things would turn around again. They always had. Because it was so demoralizing to see the continuing downward trend of stocks, I'd quit opening my monthly statements. Not a smart move.

I rushed to my file cabinet where I kept all my financial papers and took out the last couple of months' statements and opened them. The investments had gone down some, but no more than I'd expected. There was still a substantial amount in my portfolio.

I had to find out what was going on. I decided to go to Ron's office, but I didn't want to leave until Rachel and Samantha had returned. I paced the floor of the living room, back and forth, back and forth, trying to make sense of it all. But I had a terrible sense of foreboding.

It wasn't long before they came back from the therapy session. Rachel came in just long enough to tell me she thought Samantha was working hard at trying to get better. I tried to act normal, but apparently Rachel could sense that I was distracted.

"Is something wrong, Liz?" she asked.

"I hope to God not," I said. "But it's not looking good."

"What's the matter?"

I didn't usually discuss my financial situation with anyone. But I was so upset I wasn't sure if I was overreacting. Samantha had gone into her bedroom to lie down—she always came back exhausted from therapy sessions—so I signaled for Rachel to sit down and I told her what had happened.

"It's probably just a misunderstanding," she volunteered.

"But what about the disconnected phone?"

"Maybe he's moved, and you didn't get the notice of his new address and phone number."

"Okay, I'll call directory service then and see what I get."

"Good idea."

Rachel waited anxiously as I dialed information. She watched my expression as I was told his number was no longer in service and there was no new number. I shook my head in despair.

"Bad news I guess," she said.

"What am I going to do?" I was on the verge of hysteria but knew that breaking down wasn't going to do me a bit of good.

"Why don't you let me drive you over to his office?"

"I'll drive, but please come with me. I need moral support."

I went to Samantha's room and opened the door to see if she was awake. Her eyes were open so I told her I was going out for a while but would be back in time to make dinner. Then Rachel and I took off for the little office park at the corner of Battleground Avenue and Cornwallis Drive where Piedmont Investment Services, Ron's business, was located.

The offices consisted of a couple of rows of one-story condos built in colonial style. I parked in front of Ron's office and went to the door. It was locked. I peered through the window blinds that were slightly open and could see furniture but no sign of anything personal: no phones, computers, files, anything to indicate anyone used the space.

Rachel got out of the passenger seat and came up beside me. "Anything in there?"

"Just furniture. Nothing else. The guy is gone, Rachel."

"Let's see what the neighbors have to say." She went next door to an insurance office and went inside. I followed her.

"Can I help you?" the receptionist asked. She was an older woman, plumpish, white-haired and pleasant looking.

"I'm looking for Ron Pemberton who has an office next door. Do you know if he has moved his offices?" I asked.

The receptionist frowned. "A week ago we saw a U-Haul truck out front. Ron was loading his office equipment and paperwork into it. I asked him where he was going. He said he'd rented a larger office in a building downtown on Greene Street. But you're not the first person who has been looking for him. Two other people, a woman and a man, were trying to find him, too."

I looked at Rachel, and she looked at me. This didn't sound good. "Did he tell you what his new address would be?"

"No, he didn't. He said he'd give me a call once he moved in and give me his address and phone number in case anyone asked. But I haven't heard from him yet."

"Well, I'm his client and I never heard from him either," I said.

The woman chewed on her lip as if trying to decide whether to say anything or not. "There was something not quite right about that man," she said finally. "He was one of those glad handers that made you wonder if he was going to try and sell you the Brooklyn Bridge. My boss had been a client of Peter Raynor, and he thought a great deal of him, but he took his portfolio elsewhere when he got to know Ron. He didn't trust him. He must have put one over on Mr. Raynor that he turned his business over to him."

I felt mortified, for myself and for Peter who was such a trusting soul. How could he have been so duped by him? I wasn't going to tell her I was Mrs. Raynor. I thought that would only embarrass her.

I thanked her, and we returned to the car.

"What are you going to do now?" Rachel asked as she fastened her seat belt. "Do you think he really moved to Greene Street?"

"Of course not. He would have notified his clients and told the insurance agent where he was. The man is long gone." *With my money* I thought. *Maybe if I don't say it out loud, it won't be true.* But deep down inside I knew it was.

"Oh god, Liz, I'm so sorry."

I sat behind the wheel paralyzed by fear and dread. I thought I had a secure future, one that Peter had worked hard to protect and grow. Even my father's hard work had contributed to it. It seemed inconceivable that one man could destroy it. No, not destroy it, abscond with it. But hadn't there been stories in the newspaper about this happening time and again? Like every other victim, I didn't dream it could ever happen to me.

I laid my head on the steering wheel for a few minutes trying to pull myself together. Rachel put an arm around my shoulder to comfort me.

Finally I sat up. "I'm going to the police department. I don't know what else to do. Do you want me to drop you off back at my house? I don't know how long I might be."

"I'd like to go with you, unless you'd prefer I didn't."

"I'd love it if you would. I just didn't know if you had other plans this afternoon."

"Nope. I'm free. Let's go."

We drove down Battleground to Greene Street, where Ron supposedly had his new office, and parked in the municipal garage across from the police department. We looked at the different businesses but didn't see any with a sign that said Piedmont Investment Services.

We walked over to the police station and pulled open the door. I'd never been in the building before. A flat-roofed fifties-style building which also housed other municipal offices and courtrooms, the only thing that gave it away was the statue out in front of a police officer bending over and holding the hand of a small child, an attempt to put a human face on a place that dealt with the worst side of humanity.

The foyer of the building was rather large and foreboding with closed doors on every side. The only visible employee was behind a counter speaking to an agitated man. A Plexiglas shield separated the two so I couldn't hear what the woman was saying. The man was furious because his car had been towed. He was giving excuses why it had been left in the parking space for so long, but the woman apparently couldn't assuage his anger and he went stomping off through the front door.

"May I help you?" she asked when I approached the counter.

"My financial advisor has disappeared and apparently taken my life savings with him," I said.

That didn't even make her blink. I'm sure she'd dealt with far worse complaints than mine.

"I'm going to contact the Fraud Division," she said. "They'll send someone out to talk with you. Your name?"

It was only a few minutes until a side door opened and a man dressed in hinos and a polo shirt came out. "Mrs. Raynor?" he asked looking from one to the other of us.

"I'm Mrs. Raynor. This is my friend Rachel Levine. Can she come too?"

"Of course. Follow me and I'll take you back to my desk."

163

We followed him through a long hall to a room that had several desks, each piled high with file folders. Two other cops were there talking on phones. He indicated a chair beside the neatest desk and pulled another chair from across the room to place beside it. "Be seated, ladies."

He was a slightly pudgy middle-aged man who had lost much of his hair. What was left around the edges was buzz cut as if in anticipation it too would soon fall out. At least he hadn't succumbed to a comb over. The crown of his head glowed pinkish from a slight sunburn. He had a pleasant face and smile that made me feel at ease.

"I'm Detective Jacobson. Give me your personal information and then tell me your story." He pulled out a pad and prepared to take notes.

I began with the call from the bank and my attempts to reach Ron Pemberton. I told him that we'd come from his office, and it appeared that it had been cleaned out. I told him what the woman at the insurance agency next door to his office had said.

"Do you know if Mr. Pemberton has family? Have you tried to contact them?"

"I don't know a thing about his personal life. I don't know where he lived or if he had any family. I'd only talked with him about my investments. And it has been a while since I did that. My late husband was a financial advisor, and when he became ill and he knew he wouldn't survive, he turned his clients over to Ron. They'd known each other for a long time, but he was a business acquaintance, not a friend." Just talking about it was making me ill. I couldn't believe I was in the police department discussing the disappearance of my life savings.

Rachel, sitting beside me, sensed how upset I was, and she took my hand and gave it a squeeze.

"Under what name was the company registered? We can probably get the answers that way," Detective Jacobson said. His tone was sympathetic. He probably met dozens of older women who'd been swindled, but he hadn't lost the capacity to empathize with them.

"Piedmont Investment Services."

"Can you send me copies of your latest financial statements?"

"I'll do that right away."

He plucked a business card from a holder on his desk and handed it to me. "Here's my contact information and direct line. As soon as we can get a handle on this guy, we'll post him on the NCIC list. That's the National Crime Information Center. That'll get his name out there for other agencies to see. I wish I could promise you we'd get this guy and be able to restore your money, but I don't want to get your hopes up. Even if we find him, your money could already be gone. We'll do the best we can though."

He stood up signaling that the interview was over. I thanked him, and Rachel and I returned to my car.

The moment I sat in the car I fell apart. Rachel put her arm around me until I could get myself under control. It took a while to pull myself together but she sat patiently waiting for me to calm down.

"I'm not going to let that bastard ruin my life," I exclaimed. "I'm gonna get through this somehow. It may seem like the end of the world, but things can always be worse. As they say, 'It's only money.' " I'm good at spouting tired clichés as if they made me feel better.

"Good girl," Rachel said. "I know you can handle it. You're tough."

Oh, but money makes the world go round, I thought. Who am I kidding?

# CHAPTER TWENTY-THREE

Reality was beginning to set in. I was in trouble, and I didn't know where to turn. If my checks had bounced, I knew my checking account had been depleted. I had a modest amount of money in a savings account at another bank that I always thought of as my "mad money," something to fall back on in the event of a rainy day. Well, the rainy day had come in spades and it would pay the bills for a short while, but it wasn't going to last more than a couple of months or so. I had no relatives who could help me out even temporarily. I was going to end up on the street, just like Samantha had been. And of course she would end up there again as well.

Thursday morning I went to one of the employment agencies in town. I knew that most job hunting was done on the computer these days, but I had no idea how to go about it. Not only was I a novice in the high tech world, I was probably older than most employers were looking for. But I had to try. If I could find a job, perhaps I could somehow pay my bills, at least keep a roof over my head.

I ended up going to a couple of agencies. Both had long waiting lines and both, by the time I was able to talk to a counselor, informed me that there was nothing out there. The unemployment rate had reached nearly twelve percent, and even those with advanced computer skills were unable to find jobs. I was in a state of despair by the time I went home.

I called a realtor and said I wanted to put my house on the

market. I made an appointment with a woman by the name of Katherine Hawthorne for a walk through the next day. I had quite a bit of equity in the house, and I thought if I could sell it, I could invest the money and use the interest to rent a modest apartment. I'd need additional income as well, and, if nothing else, maybe I could find a part time job. Of course, once that For Sale sign went up out in front, Samantha would know something was wrong. But I'd deal with that when the time came.

I was so depressed I dreaded going to art class that evening. I didn't want to burden Jay with my bad news, but I knew that if I didn't show up, he'd call and ask why. And I needed to tell him I could no longer afford the lessons. I'd have to give up my studio at Sternberger as well. It seemed like the end of the world as I knew it.

Samantha and I sat through dinner in silence. I was the one who usually kept the conversation going, and I didn't have the heart for it today. I'm sure she sensed something was wrong, but she didn't say anything.

At class, our model that evening was an elderly woman. With the older models we learned how to strike a balance when depicting the wrinkles and sags that come with age. He didn't want us to pretty them up the way photographers sometimes do with the air brush. He wanted us to depict them with compassion and to find the beauty in aging faces.

Our model was wearing a purple dress, and I felt sure it was a reference to a line of poetry I once read that said, "When I am old, I shall wear purple." I thought *good for her.*

As I painted, I felt age bearing down on me. I was probably twenty-five or thirty years younger than our model, but it seemed as if the past couple of days had added years. I wasn't as resilient as I used to be. Or maybe I never was; I just hadn't been tested like this before.

167

As the class drew to a close, Jay came by and whispered "Coffee?" What I really wanted was a good stiff drink, but then I wouldn't be able to drive home. I nodded and proceeded to put away my art supplies. I wondered when I'd be able to use them again.

In Jay's truck on the way to Ganache restaurant, he said he'd had the urge for a piece of their dreamy chocolate raspberry cake. He noticed I was so quiet and asked why.

Before I could say a word, I began to cry. Quietly at first, then finally in gulping sobs. All my anxiety and confusion was bubbling over and I couldn't control it.

He pulled over to the side of Elm Street and stopped. Putting his arms around me he said, "What is it, Liz? What's the matter?"

I told him briefly what had happened the last two days. It came tumbling out in between the hiccups that my crying had triggered. "I don't know what I'm going to do!" I bawled.

"Look," he said, "we'll figure this out together. You don't have to feel like you're in this alone."

"But I am alone!" I cried. "You can give me moral support, but you can't restore my money or find me a job or sell my house. Nobody can do that. I'm going to end up on the street!"

"No, you're not," he said. "I won't let that happen. We'll think of something."

I looked up into his kind eyes. Maybe he couldn't restore my money, but it meant the world that he was there for me, that somebody cared. I fished a tissue out of my purse and wiped my eyes. "Sorry to dump on you. I just feel overwhelmed."

"It's no wonder." He smiled and leaned over and kissed me. "Don't you think a piece of chocolate raspberry cake might give you a little lift right now?"

"If I eat a piece of cake every time I get stressed, I'll blow up like a balloon."

"I'm not suggesting you make a habit of it. But just this time?"

"Sure, why not." I pulled out my compact and looked at myself. It was not a pretty sight. I patted on a little makeup and added some lipstick so I didn't look like the walking dead as Jay drove on to the Ganache parking lot.

As we ate our cake and drank our coffee I told him in more detail about my visit to the police and my experience at the employment agencies.

"I have a realtor coming tomorrow to see about putting my house on the market."

He put his fork down and frowned. "Oh, no, Liz. Surely you aren't going to sell that beautiful house you put so much work into."

"I don't have a choice. Either I sell it or the bank is going to repossess it. If I can get as much as I hope for it, I'll invest it and use the income to rent a little apartment. But I'll have to work as well to pay the rest of my bills—if I can ever find a job."

He shook his head. "This is unbelievable. You read about such things, but you never think it's going to happen to you or a loved one."

The "loved one" statement was like balm to my pain.

"What are you going to do about Samantha?" He was scraping the last bit of cake off his plate. I'd already consumed all of mine.

"I'll take her with me wherever I go. At least until she can get on her feet again."

He took me back to the parking garage where I'd parked and waited until I was safely in my car. As I'd gotten out of the truck he said, "We'll figure this all out, Liz. Just remember you are not alone in this."

The realtor, Katherine, came the next day and I walked her

through the house. I'd had to break the news to Samantha before she came, but she said nothing as usual. She barely touched her lunch however.

Katherine came across as one of those brusque no-nonsense women who was all business. No touchy-feely, sympathetic words from her. And she looked like the headmistress of an exclusive girls' school: steel gray hair pulled back in a French twist, black suit that couldn't hide her ample frame, old fashioned white blouse with a bow at the neck. After we'd done the tour, we sat down at the dining table to discuss her findings.

"You've done a nice job on your renovations," she said, "and this is usually a very popular area as far as home sales go. But you have to realize the market is in terrible shape right now. You can't expect to get what you could have sold it for a year ago. And you have some drawbacks too. You only have two bedrooms and that is definitely a minus. Your kitchen is quite nice, but you know everyone wants granite countertops and stainless steel appliances these days."

We had remodeled the kitchen before these became "must haves" but frankly I didn't think they would have blended well with the craftsman style of our old home anyway. I wondered why everyone thought they were imperative.

She mentioned some other minor things that needed attention. I'll admit I hadn't kept up the maintenance the way that Peter had, but these were easily fixable.

She then gave me a figure that she thought would be a good sales price to start out with, and my heart sank. With all our renovations, even though we did much of the work ourselves, I wouldn't get much of a profit in the end. Only because we had lived in it as long as we had and our mortgage had been paid down enough would I get some cash that I could invest. But not as much as I thought.

I signed a contract with her for ninety days though I'd heard the average time a house was on the market these days was about six months. I'd see how much effort she put into showing it before I decided to renew her contract.

Samantha had stayed in her bedroom during this time. I don't think she wanted to hear our discussion. I knew she had to be feeling terribly vulnerable.

I knocked on her door, and she said to come in.

She was lying in the bed staring at the ceiling.

"Samantha," I said, "I need to explain all this to you. I'd hoped I could shield you from this bad news, but I can't do that any longer. Well, there's no easy way to say this so I'll just say it. My financial advisor ran off with all my investment money. That means I have very little left. If I can sell this house, I can use that money to find us a small apartment. And I'll have to get a job to pay the everyday expenses. I'm so sorry this had to happen while you're staying with me, but I know we'll work it all out. You are not going to be out on the street again."

She'd continued to look at the ceiling as I spoke, and a long silence followed.

Finally she looked at me. "I'm nothing but bad luck. Everything has gone wrong since I came here."

"It has nothing at all to do with you, Samantha. This is a bad time for everybody right now. And, yes, both of us have had setbacks. But it's not your fault. We're going to get through this together."

"You don't have to take care of me. As soon as my leg is healed, I'll leave."

I squeezed her hand. "I don't want you to. I need your support. Just by being here you give me the courage to go on. I can see how you've persevered, and it gives me hope that I can too."

She gave me a wan smile. "Really?"

"Really."

171

# CHAPTER TWENTY-FOUR

The increasingly warm spring days and the eruption of bloom all over town didn't lessen my unhappiness; it only served to heighten my sense of loss. I felt I was in a holding pattern: going regularly to the employment agencies to no avail, waiting for the almost nonexistent potential buyers to go through my house. I'd paid rent through April at Sternberger so I had a couple more weeks I could use my studio. I spent more and more time there trying to escape my woes. I could forget for a little while at a time when I became engrossed in a painting, but reality would return in full force each time I left.

Jay and I had occasional dinners together. But we never had a chance for intimate time alone. With Samantha at my house and Brian at his, we couldn't spend weekends together. I wondered if we ever would again. His teaching schedule didn't permit him much free time during the day, but once in a while we could spend an hour or two together at places like Bicentennial Gardens where spring was in all its glory.

Rachel was very supportive and worried about me. I had told her I could no longer afford to go out to lunch with her, but she insisted on taking me as her guest a couple of times.

"Rachel, you can't afford this any more than I can," I said as we drove to Café Europa.

"I just sold a short story to *Glimmer Train*," she said. "You probably haven't heard of it, but it's one of the most prestigious literary magazines. And they actually pay a decent fee. So this is my way of celebrating."

"That's fantastic," I said. "You're really on your way."

"I doubt that. But agents do look at these magazines and sometimes contact authors they like to see if they have any books in the works."

"Do you?" She hadn't mentioned any.

"I just started one. Barely have gotten into it. But I think this is what I need to do now. There are so few markets for short stories."

We had reached the parking deck behind the Cultural Arts Center and Rachel turned into it. I waited till we were parked and walking toward the stairs before I asked her, "I'm curious. What's it about?"

"If you don't mind, I'd rather not talk about it. I sort of feel like if I do, it might jinx it."

"That's fine. I just want the very first copy when it's published."

"You got it, kiddo." She smiled broadly, and we did a high five.

I hadn't called Meredith recently. I found her attitude disturbing the last time I talked to her, and I'd just about crossed her off my list.

But she called me one night to chat. For the longest time I tried to sound upbeat and was very vague about what I'd been doing. I just didn't want to hear any negative stuff coming out of her.

Finally she said, "Something's wrong, Liz. I know you too well, and I can tell that you're unhappy. What is it?"

"Oh, you know, the little daily aggravations."

"Bullshit. I can tell that it's much more than that. Now are you going to tell me what's going on, or do I have to come over there and beat it out of you?"

That's Meredith. Once she gets started on a subject, she's as tenacious as all get out. She won't let up until you tell her.

"My financial advisor has absconded with all my money."

"*What?* Oh my god, Liz, what are you going to do?"

"Well, I've put my house on the market, only no one is coming to look at it."

"And where will you go if you sell it?"

"I'll find an inexpensive apartment. And I need to find a job."

"And what about Samantha?"

"She'll stay with me until she's able to be on her own."

"You are one helluva lady. I know I've been hard on you about taking her in, but, honestly, Liz, I do admire you. You know I make the big bucks, and I'd very much like to help you out. I can give you what you need till you find a job. Consider it a loan. Please let me do that."

I was astonished. I'd been so angry over some of her remarks lately that I was beginning to feel as if we had nothing in common and wondered how our friendship had lasted as long as it did. Now she was willing to give me unlimited help. I guess I'd misjudged her badly. Even when you think you know people well, sometimes they can surprise the hell out of you.

"I appreciate that very much, Meredith. Right now I'm able to get by, and I hope the house will sell before I run out of funds. But should I find myself in trouble, I'll definitely call you." I hoped and prayed I wouldn't have to. I still didn't want to be in her debt.

"Be sure to do that," she said. "And please keep me up to date with what's going on, won't you? I'm going to be so worried about you."

"Thanks, Meredith. I will, I promise."

Even though I had several people to lean on now both emotionally and financially, I wondered how desperate I'd have to be before asking for their help. I wasn't used to depending on others to get by.

I decided I couldn't wait until the house had sold to look for an apartment. I couldn't do anything until the actual sale, of course, but I wanted to get a sense of what was available and at what price. I'd never lived in anything but a house, so I didn't know what to expect.

Jay went with me when he had the time. Because of the recession every complex had vacancies and all kinds of incentives from a free month's rent on up. But I was still unprepared for the cost to rent a decent apartment in a safe part of town. And the fact I needed two bedrooms made the rent even higher. I wondered if the money from the sale of my house would be sufficient. A low selling price meant less money to invest and less interest to live on.

Katherine brought one or two clients through each week. We tried to schedule the showings during the time I took Samantha to her therapy sessions. Otherwise it would be too difficult to get her out of the house each time.

I talked to the detective about once a week to see if any progress had been made tracking down Ron Pemberton, but it was as if Pemberton had disappeared into thin air. He was probably living it up on some Caribbean Island—and with my money!

Samantha was making progress. At first she couldn't put any weight on the broken leg, but gradually she was allowed to put more and more weight on it. She'd graduated from a walker to crutches, but she still had to scoot up and down the steps.

Soon I had to pack up all my books and paint supplies at Sternberger to take home on the last day of April. I had dreaded this almost as much as selling my home. It had been a place of healing and growth, easing the pain of the loss of Peter and nurturing my desire to become a better painter. Rachel helped me pack up. I think she felt as bad as I did. I told her that since my house was so close, she'd have to come to lunch now and then. She said she'd love to.

We loaded the boxes along with the easel into my car. Rachel hugged me and said that Sternberger wouldn't be the same without me. I knew that was true because she and I were the only ones who were there regularly during the day. It was going to be a lonesome place when she was there alone.

My classes had been paid for through April, and the last one was that evening. I'd gone a little early to tell Jay I could no longer attend, but Jay insisted I continue anyway. "But doesn't a part of the fee go to the Art Alliance?" I asked.

"I just won't put you on the list. They won't know if there's one more person than the list says. I've done enough extra stuff for them without charge. I don't feel a bit guilty about it." I was helping him to set up the easels that had been stored away. Maintenance had taken them all down to lay some new vinyl tiles on the worn floor.

"If you're sure it's okay it would mean a lot. It hurt so much to give up Sternberger. At least I could keep my hand in."

"Why don't you paint in your dining room?" He had just finished setting up the last easel, and we went to sit side by side on the platform.

"Because I have to keep the place spotless in case my realtor drags somebody through."

"Bummer." He traced the outline of a floor tile with his finger, deep in thought.

"Yeah, especially because the people are few and far between. But I never know much in advance when they're coming."

He frowned and shook his head. "I can't believe you're going through all this. I wish there was more I could do."

"Your moral support means everything to me. Just keep on

being there for me."

He hugged me. "You can count on it."

I had just enough money to make my May mortgage payment. If my house didn't sell soon, I would be in deep trouble. I decided to wait till close to the end of the month before going to the loan officer to explain my position. I prayed the bank would give me some latitude if things didn't get any better. I had nightmares of being escorted out of my home by a deputy when it went into foreclosure.

Katherine called me the end of the first week in May to say she'd gotten an offer. She wanted to come over and discuss it with me. From the tone of her voice I didn't dare get my hopes up. She didn't exactly sound elated.

Samantha went to her room when the doorbell rang. I'd told her Katherine was coming, and I think she was in denial about the situation, trying to avoid any discussion about our future options.

The realtor bustled in with her briefcase and plopped down on the sofa beside me.

"It's not a great offer," she said pulling out papers. "In fact it's almost insulting. But it's up to you, of course. If you feel you must get this resolved, you might want to consider it."

My spirits plunged. "So what did they say?"

"They're offering thirty thousand below your asking price." She dropped the papers on the coffee table as if they were burning her fingers.

"That's ridiculous. Are they serious?" I was angry that anyone thought they could take advantage of me that way.

"I guess they feel people are desperate and they can get a steal."

"I'm not that bad off. At least not yet. Do you think they'll make a counter offer if I came down a little?" I was feeling a lot more desperate than I let on.

"We'll see. But, frankly, I think they're interested in a fire sale. They may come up a bit but not much. Do you want to make a counter offer?" She tapped her finger on the papers, restless to be off to her next appointment.

"At this point I'll go down five thousand. They'll probably laugh at that. But I don't want to get in a bidding war with them."

"Okay. I'll go see what I can do." Katherine stood up, shoved the papers back in the briefcase, and shook my hand. "Things should be picking up. They usually do around the time that school is out. So if you can hang in there, you might get some out-of-towners who are moving here."

I walked with her to the door feeling even more discouraged than I had fifteen minutes earlier. The timing for selling my house couldn't have been worse with the housing market in such disarray.

"I'll call you as soon as I hear anything," she called back over her shoulder as she hurried down the steps.

I didn't expect much to come of that.

Samantha shuffled out of the bedroom when she heard the door close.

"Have you sold it?" From her tone I couldn't tell whether she wanted it to be sold or not.

"I don't think so. Someone wanted to give me a whole lot less than it's worth."

She looked down at the floor. "I guess that's not good." She was silent for a while. I could tell she wanted to say something but was reluctant to do so. Finally she spoke in a soft voice still looking at the floor. "So what happens now?"

I had no idea what was going to happen, but I didn't want to alarm her. "Something will turn up. I'm sure of it."

When she looked at me I could tell she didn't believe me for a minute.

# CHAPTER TWENTY-FIVE

A couple of days later Katherine came back to tell me the couple had raised their offer by five thousand dollars.

"They want twenty-five thousand off? No way. I'm not giving my house away."

Furious, I wanted to meet the couple and tell them what I thought of them taking advantage of a poor widow lady. And then I almost laughed. Get real, Liz, I told myself. They probably don't know I'm a widow, and if I were in their shoes, I'd probably try to wheel and deal too. *You can't take this personally.*

"I think you made the right decision. And I don't think they're willing to come up any more. Let's just write them off. I feel sure you can do better than that."

She stowed the papers from the offer in her briefcase and gave me a pat on the arm as she left. "Don't be discouraged," she said. But how could I help it?

That afternoon, feeling totally at loose ends, I decided to paint at my dining room table. I was tired of trying to keep an immaculate house. If somebody wanted to view it, I could shove everything in a closet in a hurry. I went through my snapshots of children that I'd used as subjects before I got into Jay's class. I found one of a child working on a sand castle on the beach that I liked. I brought in the box of art supplies that I hadn't unpacked since I brought them home from Sternberger and dug out brushes, watercolors, paper, and palette. I covered the dining table with a plastic cloth and brought in a bowl of water and a drawing board.

I was taping the paper to the board when Samantha came out of her bedroom.

"Can I watch?" she asked.

"Sure, Samantha. This is what I did every morning when I went over to my studio. Since I can't afford it any more, I thought I'd try to work here."

"I used to draw and paint some."

"Really? I had no idea. Do you want to paint today? I've got another board you can use."

"Yes, please. I'd like to." She settled herself in a chair on the opposite side of the table. "Can I use one of your photos? I need something to work from."

"Of course." I handed her the box of photos and went to look for the other drawing board that was in my bedroom closet.

By the time I returned to the dining room she had picked out a scene taken at Holden Beach of dunes and sea oats with the ocean in the distance.

"I like this," she said holding it up. "I don't know how to draw people."

"Excellent," I said. I had lots of tubes of watercolor, at least two of almost every hue. I'd stocked up during sales because I always worried about running out of a certain color in the middle of a painting. So I pulled out all the shades of brown, tan, yellow, blue and green that I thought she would need, several brushes of the appropriate size and brought her a bowl of water from the kitchen and an old plate to mix her colors on. I helped her tape a piece of paper to the board. I bought heavy watercolor stock that didn't need to be soaked in water before being used.

It was very companionable as we sat on opposite sides of the table working on our paintings. I would glance at Samantha every now and then and was amazed at how absorbed she was. I

181

was sorry I hadn't thought of this sooner, but I had no inkling she was the least bit interested in painting. I knew she was bored with TV and, though she loved to read, that got old too. I never could think of any way to entertain her. Now it seemed as if I'd accidentally hit on something that she liked to do.

It was one o'clock before I realized that we hadn't eaten lunch. I cleaned off my brushes, put the caps on my tubes of paint and got up and stretched. I walked around the table to see how Samantha was doing.

I'd misjudged her and expected some child-like rendering of sand and sea. I was totally unprepared for the nuanced rendering of sand dunes and waving sea oats. The sky was beautifully done with floating clouds that looked real instead of like cartoons. Samantha had real talent!

"That's lovely," I said. "Have you had art lessons?"

"I took art in high school before I dropped out. My teacher was really good, and she encouraged me. But I really haven't done any painting since."

"Well, you are very talented Samantha. We need to keep you doing it."

Samantha's face was glowing. Such a change from the somber look she'd had for so long. "I'm really happy when I paint. I'm so glad you let me."

I realized that if I hadn't been forced to give up my studio, I never would have discovered Samantha's interest. Maybe this would be some kind of breakthrough to draw her out. I couldn't wait to tell Jay about this.

We took a lunch break and then both returned to our painting. She completed three pictures that day, albeit small ones. Fortunately I had a good supply of paper because it's quite expensive, and I wasn't sure I could afford to buy much now. I hoped I could get some kind of discount through Jay's contacts.

It was Thursday, and I had art class that evening. I wished I could have taken Samantha with me but several things made it impossible. First she couldn't stand at an easel until her leg healed. I wasn't sure she was ready to paint from live models yet, and I couldn't expect Jay to take her on for free.

We had a model that we'd had several times before, a young, wholesome looking woman with bright red hair and freckled face. I wouldn't call her beautiful, but she had a pixie quality that was a delight to try and capture. It was always a special challenge to get the right shade of red that made her hair look natural rather than dyed. And the freckles were challenging too. If overdone, they looked like paint specks. It took a light touch to make them seem real. I always enjoyed the process of painting her.

Jay and I went downstairs to Café Europa after class for our coffee.

"I got the most wonderful surprise today," I told him after we'd ordered.

"Did someone make an offer on the house?" That had been the topic of so much discussion it was no wonder it was the first thing he thought of.

"The only offer I've gotten was so far off the mark I won't even consider it. No, I decided to heck with worrying about my realtor bringing people through. I have to paint. So I'm working in the dining room. I figure I can shove it in a closet if I get a call from Katherine."

"I'm glad to hear that. With everything else you have to give up, I didn't want you to be denied the opportunity to paint." Jay, more than anyone, knew how much it meant to my well-being.

"Well, I was all set up to begin, and Samantha came in and asked if she could paint too. And, Jay, the girl is talented! I had no idea."

Jay's face lit up. "I'll be damned. That sounds like something we can nurture."

I knew that he would be as excited as I was. "I really think it will draw her out. She desperately needs some positive experiences in her life."

"I'd like to help her out. Could she take a course over here?" Jay asked.

"I can't afford to pay for it." That seemed to be my answer to everything these days.

"Oh, yeah, that's true. Let me think." His expression got very serious as he drew circles on the table top with his finger.

The waiter brought the coffee, and we both sipped, lost in thought.

"I've got an idea. Why don't you bring her out to my place on Saturday afternoon and maybe I can work with her."

My heart swelled with gratitude. I never would have asked him to do such a thing.

"What about Brian?" I asked. I knew Jay had felt Brian could resent our relationship, and he had carefully kept us apart up until now.

"It's time you two met each other. I should have done it sooner, but I guess I was chicken. I can't put my life on hold forever for Brian's benefit."

I reached up and pulled his head toward me and kissed him hard on the lips. I didn't care who was watching. "You are the best."

He smiled. "The best what? Kisser?"

"That, too."

# CHAPTER TWENTY-SIX

Saturday afternoon Samantha and I drove to Jay's home. I think she was a little nervous about the trip. I know I was nervous about meeting Brian.

Jay came out the door as soon as we pulled in the driveway. "Hello, hello," he said, opening the door for Samantha. "Can I help you out?"

"My crutches are in the back seat."

He got them out, helped Samantha scoot off the car seat, and made sure she was steady on her crutches before he came around to my side. I was already out of the car and we followed him into the house. Luckily there was only one step to maneuver and with me in front and Jay in back to catch her if she fell, she managed it with her crutches. I tended to hover over her like a mother hen. I couldn't bear the thought of her hurting herself again.

A young man with a striking resemblance to Jay was in the living room. He was slender like his dad, and his nose was a carbon copy, large but rather noble looking, I thought. His slightly auburn hair was probably the color Jay's once was before it turned gray and had the same unruly curl, though his was much longer than his dad's. He got up and came toward us. If Samantha's appearance seemed odd to him, he never showed it.

"Liz and Samantha, this is Brian." Jay put his arm around his son like a proud dad.

We nodded and Brian extended his hand to shake ours. He

seemed to be well mannered. It was hard to imagine he'd given his father so much grief.

"Have a seat," Jay said, gesturing toward the sofa. Once we were seated he initiated the conversation. "So, Samantha, I understand you love to paint."

She smiled, probably the first time Jay had ever seen her smile. "I do."

"Well, we'll get you set up with a place in my studio. It's quite large, so we can put up a table for you that won't be disturbed. Liz can bring you out on Saturdays, and you can leave anything there you want." I had no idea he'd meant to do this on a permanent basis; I'd thought the invitation was for today only. I was astounded at his generosity.

"That's nice." Her smile became even wider. I'd never seen her so happy before.

"So, Brian," I said, wanting to bring him into the conversation, "I guess it's not too long before school is out. What year are you?"

"A junior." I could tell from the tone of his voice that school was not his favorite subject. I noticed Jay scowl slightly and decided I'd stumbled onto a sore subject. But it was a little late to change subjects now. I'd try to get out of it gracefully.

"So one more year. Are you looking forward to graduation?"

"I'm kind of thinking about taking the GED and enlisting in the army. I'll be seventeen in September." I must have misunderstood what Jay told me. I thought that wasn't a consideration until after graduation. No wonder his dad was scowling.

"Your dad said you were thinking about it. So you're serious now?"

"Yeah. Granddad has been talking to me about it. He's an army guy. He thinks it would be good for me."

I looked at Jay to gauge his reaction. From the way he

compressed his lips I could tell he was trying hard not to say anything.

"Aren't you worried about going somewhere like Afghanistan?"

"I'm hoping I can sign up for training that would keep me out of there. Or at least out of the front lines. Since I'm in the culinary arts program at Weaver, I'm hoping I can get a job as a cook. But I'll take whatever they give me."

"Well, it seems to me it's just as dangerous behind the front lines." I knew as soon as I said it I was digging myself in deeper and deeper.

He started to pick at a fingernail. I had a hunch he'd been around on this subject with his father. I should have kept my mouth shut. Finally he said, "It's a chance I'm willing to take."

I racked my mind for a way to change the subject, but Jay spoke up and said, "Why don't we show Samantha the studio?"

The three of us went out to the building behind the house. Brian stayed in the living room.

Samantha's eyes opened wide when she saw all the paintings around the room. I prayed that Jay had done as promised and kept the one of me out of sight. I hadn't yet seen the completed portrait, and I didn't know if I would get a chance today. With all the upheaval in my life I'd forgotten about it. But now I was very curious to see it.

"These are all your paintings?" Samantha asked Jay.

"They are. Just a small part of what I've done."

"Wow. They are great. I've never learned how to paint people."

"Well, maybe I can help you with that. Look over here. I put up this card table for you. This will be your space. I have plenty of paints and brushes, and I'll let you choose what you want and keep it here for your use. There's a sink over there for water, and I've given you a palette to mix your colors on."

Samantha hopped over on her crutches and sat down at the

table, looking around at her supplies. She was glowing. Jay had already taped a piece of paper to a board and he brought a bowl of water from the sink for her. "Why don't you just play around with the paints now. I have some things I'd like to show Liz."

Samantha went to work and Jay took my hand and led me into a storage room at the back of the studio.

"I want to show you something," he said as he pulled a chain to turn on the overhead light. A stack of framed paintings leaned against the wall. He went through them till he found one near the bottom and pulled it out. It was the completed portrait he did of me, beautifully framed in cherry wood with a deep linen mat. Even though I was a tiny bit embarrassed still, I thought it was the best picture he'd ever done, at least of the ones I'd seen. I felt so honored.

"But why did you frame it?" I asked. "I hope you aren't going to display it anywhere."

"I'm not. I wouldn't want to embarrass you, even though I don't think you should *be* embarrassed about it. But it deserved to be framed, even hidden away back here. It's one of my favorite paintings ever."

I put my arms around his neck. "I think so too. I wish I were gutsy enough to say go on and display it; I don't care what anyone thinks—but I don't believe I can do it. I'm sorry."

He kissed me tenderly. "I understand, my dear. It'll be our special secret."

Jay asked Samantha if she wanted to stay a little while, and she said she would like to finish one piece. She was working on a beach scene similar to the one she did that day with me. We left Samantha painting at her table and strolled back to the house. On the way, Jay said he'd start giving her instructions the following weekend. "Why don't you plan to paint, too? You can work on whatever you want while I help her."

"That's unbelievably generous of you, Jay."

"You know I love to teach. And since she's connected to you, it gives me extra pleasure to work with her."

Brian was still in the living room when we returned.

"What happened to Samantha?" he asked. He was sprawled on the sofa, one leg thrown over the arm of it reading a *People* magazine.

"She's doing some painting. I'm going to give her lessons on Saturday afternoons from now on."

Brian scowled, the first he'd let his pleasant mask slip. "I thought we were going to work on my motorcycle together. That's the only day I have off work."

Jay turned to me. "Brian's been working at a fast food restaurant after school Friday night and on Sundays. He'll go full time when school is out." Then he spoke to his son. "I'll help you Saturday mornings."

"But you know I don't get up early because I have to work so late."

Now it was Jay's turn to frown. "We'll work something out, Brian. I'd rather not discuss it now."

Brian threw down the magazine, shot his father an angry look, and stomped up the stairs.

Jay rubbed his forehead as though he felt a headache coming on and flopped down in a chair. "I'm sorry, Liz. Sometimes things go smoothly with him and other times not so much."

"Look," I said, "I don't want to cause any friction between you two. Maybe we should forget about the lessons for Samantha." I sat down on the sofa vacated by Brian.

"No way. I could tell how excited she was at the prospect of lessons. Maybe this could draw her out a little. Anyway, I'm not going to let Brian act this way. And, besides, I've always hated the damn motorcycle. I worry every time he gets on it. I was trying to mend our fences when I said I'd help him fix it."

"Well, I don't want us to be the ones that mess that up for you."

"You're not. We have a lot of baggage between us right now. Maybe that's the usual with fathers and sons, I don't know. But I'll work on it as best I can. If I can't bring him around, then I can only hope that as he matures, he'll figure out I'm not such a bad guy after all. I may be an old man before that happens, but I'll keep on trying."

I didn't see Brian again the rest of the time we were there. On the way home Samantha was as chatty as I'd ever known her to be.

"That's so great that Jay's going to let me paint there. I always wanted to take lessons, outside of school I mean, but I could never afford it."

"He's an excellent teacher. Maybe I'll do some painting, too, when we're there."

"Oh, are you giving up your Thursday evening class?"

"No, I don't think so." For one thing, I wanted to paint the models that Jay lined up for us on Thursdays. And after class seemed to be about the only time Jay and I could be alone for a while. "But a little more practice on Saturdays would be good for me."

# CHAPTER TWENTY-SEVEN

I heard from the detective at the police department that so far they'd been unable to run down Ron Pemberton. They would keep trying, of course, but a lot of good that did me. If I didn't get a decent bid on my house pretty soon, I'd be in a world of trouble.

Katherine Hawthorne, my realtor, brought only an occasional potential buyer to view the house. I usually was in the middle of a painting and had to frantically gather up my things and stuff them in a closet, praying they wouldn't look inside it. But none of them made an offer. I didn't know whether to switch realtors or stick with her. I knew that times were bad and it wasn't her fault that my house didn't sell. She seemed to be doing her best. After much soul searching I decided to stay with her and sign another contract.

The only good thing that had happened was that Samantha had been able to give up the crutches and walk almost normally. She did exercises at home that the therapist had shown her, and she had only a slight limp that with time and effort she hoped would go away.

The weather had turned very hot, but I kept the thermostat at eighty because I couldn't afford high utility bills. It was the middle of June and, without a miracle, Samantha and I would be out on the street soon. I'd had no luck at all trying to find a job. And I wasn't proud. I applied for any job that I could conceivably do from greeter at the ubiquitous mammoth discount center to office manager at the neighborhood stationary store. I was beginning to wonder if both of us would be back at the homeless shelter before the summer was over.

When Jay and I went out for coffee after class the second week of June, I was feeling as low as I'd ever felt.

I didn't want to discuss my situation, hoping foolishly if I didn't talk about it, it would all miraculously go away. But Jay kept probing.

"Have any lookers this week?" he asked as we settled at our table at the Green Bean.

"Can't we talk about something else?" I had a headache and was feeling cross.

He looked at me sternly. "Liz, you can't hide your head in the sand. You have to be proactive about your situation."

That made me angry. "Proactive? What on earth do you think I've been doing? I've probably sent out a thousand resumes. I've cut back my spending to the bare minimum. There's not a damn thing I can do about selling the house except cross my fingers and hope for the best. What would you have me do?" I could feel my face getting warm, and I realized I'd spoken so loudly the people at the next table were staring at me.

Jay looked at me calmly as if I were being completely rational. "Have you planned for what you'll do if you lose the house?" he said softly, bringing our conversation back to an intimate level.

His words hit me like a slap in the face. I really hadn't thought about it. I didn't *want* to think about it. I couldn't accept that it was almost a certainty, inevitable. I excused myself and went to the ladies' room where I could have a meltdown in private. I sat in a stall and bawled my eyes out.

When I looked in the mirror, I looked terrible: puffy, reddened eyes, tear-streaked cheeks. I washed my face, repaired my makeup, and went back out to rejoin Jay.

"Feeling better?" he asked.

"A little. But you're right. I have avoided thinking about it because I don't know what to do. I get panicky every time, so I simply put it out of my mind."

"Well, I have a suggestion for you. If you have to move out, and that's going to happen whether or not you sell your house, you know, why don't you and Samantha move in with us?"

I looked at him in astonishment. "You're kidding me, right? You don't have room for us."

"Oh, but I do. I have three bedrooms, one of which is an unused guest bedroom which Samantha can have. I can get a double bed for my bedroom." He raised his eyebrows in question.

I had never anticipated that he would make such a generous offer. But it could be complicated. "What about Brian, Jay? Wouldn't he resent that? I know you're making progress in your relationship, and I don't want to interfere with that."

"Brian's got to learn that he's not the center of the universe. And he seems determined to join the army which he can do in October. So if you came, it would only mean two or three months before he leaves. I'm really serious about this, Liz."

I took a sip of my coffee which had gotten cold while I was in the ladies' room. "I'll have to think about it. But it's lovely of you to ask."

He picked up my left hand and squeezed it. "I can't think of anything nicer than having you live with me."

"There's one thing," I said. "As long as Brian's there, if I do come we must be discreet. It would be like throwing gasoline on the fire if we flaunt our relationship in front of him. I'm not crazy about sleeping with Samantha, but for the time being I think I must."

Jay scowled and chewed on his lip as he thought about that. "I hate having to pussyfoot around him all the time, but I suppose you're right. At least it's only for a short time."

193

"And if he changes his mind and decides to finish school?"

Jay made a face. "That's a tough one, Liz. But we can work it out when and if it happens."

I felt terrible, like I was putting him on the spot if we came to live with him. "Maybe we ought to wait and see what he does for sure."

"And in the meantime, what? Where are you and Samantha going to live?"

The certainty of my future was bearing down on me. I couldn't seem to grasp the idea I would soon be homeless. The idea was appalling. I just shook my head and said, "I don't know, Jay. I just don't know."

"Well, *I* know. You're going to stay with me, and no argument about it." His look was determined and brooked no dissent.

"What would I do with all my furniture?" I asked. "I have family pieces that I can't bear to give away. I know it's selfish of me to think about that under the circumstances, but it seems that's all I would have left of my former life."

"I have space up over the garage. I put stairs and a floor in some years ago so I could use it for storage, but there's still plenty of room there. I'm sure it would accommodate your things."

I couldn't help but smile at him. "You've thought it all out, haven't you? You are such a generous man, Jay."

He picked up my hand and brought it to his lips for a kiss. "I wouldn't do this for anyone but you, Liz. I hate what's happening to you, but it's brought us closer together. I can't help but be a bit thankful for that."

I took his hand in both of mine and held it tight. "I don't know how I got so lucky."

"I think I'm the lucky one."

It was the next day that circumstances seemed to turn in my

194

favor. Katherine called and said she wanted to meet with me right away. "I have an offer," she said. "It's not what you're asking, but I think you might be interested." That's all she would tell me on the phone.

I didn't know if I dare let my hopes rise or not. And it would be bittersweet in any event. If I could sell the house, I'd have some money to live on till I could find a job, a lot better than losing it to the bank. But either way it was gone.

That morning an article in the newspaper told of a family of four who had lost everything in a fire. When interviewed, however, they claimed that they felt blessed that they all were alive and well. I had to remember that houses were just houses and things were just things. If we came out of a situation unscathed, that was the important thing. Houses and furniture can be replaced.

I prepared a pitcher of tea and a plate of cookies for Katherine's arrival. She came bustling in as usual but had a smile on her face for the first time. I poured two glasses of tea and we sat down at the dining table where she pulled out a sheaf of papers from her briefcase.

"I have a bid here that's fifteen thousand under your asking price. And they want you to pay the closing costs. I'll be honest with you, Liz. I think that's as good as it's going to get. My advice would be to take it."

"Don't you think I should make a counter offer?"

She picked up the sheaf of papers and tapped them together on the table to straighten them. She was not a hand holder and never tried to soften the truth. "Under most circumstances I would say yes. But the situation is so dire right now, I think you should just take it. Don't give these buyers a chance to slip away."

I didn't have to think about it for long. The closing fees would probably be another five thousand meaning I'd get twenty thousand less than I hoped for. I did mental calculations in my head. That wouldn't give me enough money to rent my own place for any length of time; I'd soon go through my funds if I couldn't find a job. But it would provide me enough to pay personal expenses for myself and Samantha and help Jay with utility bills and food if we moved in with him. I could see that as a temporary arrangement until I could find work.

"Okay, let's do it," I said.

"Good girl. I think you've made the right decision."

We went through the papers, and I signed and initialed everything.

"They've been pre-approved for the loan, so I don't think we'll run into any problems," Katherine said getting up and stuffing the contract back in her briefcase. "I'll be in touch." And she breezed out of the house. She had barely touched her tea.

Samantha came out of her bedroom where she always retreated when guests came.

Her eyes looked frightened. "I heard what she said. What are we going to do now?"

I hadn't shared much with Samantha about my plans. But now that things were going forward, I needed to bring her into the loop.

"My friend Jay has asked us to stay with him until we can afford to make better arrangements. As soon as I can find a job, we'll get our own apartment."

"He wants *me?* Like, he hardly knows me."

"He knows that I want you with me. We'll have to share a bedroom if you don't mind that."

"I won't mind at all. And does this mean I can paint in his studio any time I want?"

"Absolutely."

Her face lit up. "Really? Wow!"

# CHAPTER TWENTY-EIGHT

Meredith called me that weekend.

"Honestly, Liz, you never call me anymore. What gives?"

"I'm sorry, Meredith. I'm so focused on my problems right now I can't seem to think past them. I didn't intend to hurt you. I've just been feeling overwhelmed."

"So tell me what's going on. I offered to help you out financially."

"You did. And that was very generous of you. But I think I'll soon have things under control."

"Well, tell me for heaven's sake. Did they find the guy who made off with the money?"

I'd been standing in the kitchen going through my cupboards trying to figure out what I could get rid of when I moved. I couldn't possibly take everything with me. But I figured this was going to be a long conversation, so I moved to the dining room and sat at the table.

"Don't I wish. No, but I think I've sold the house providing everything goes through."

"Well, my gosh, what are you going to do then?"

I knew I was going to catch hell for not telling her more about my relationship with Jay, but it was too late now. "I'm going to move in with a friend—my art teacher."

I cringed as I waited for her reaction, and I wasn't disappointed.

"*What?* You've been holding out on me, girl. I want to hear this story—now!"

And so I told her all about Jay. However, I did leave out the painting he did of me. I knew she would tease me unmercifully if she knew about it.

She interrupted my monologue with an occasional "good girl" and "can't believe it" and when I finished said, "And you couldn't have shared this with me sooner?"

I figured that whatever I said it was going to make her mad. So I just said it. "I'm sorry, Meredith. It is such a private thing. And I wasn't convinced it was going to last. I didn't feel like talking about it until I was sure about him. Maybe I thought I'd jinx it."

Instead of being angry, she laughed. "You mean the way I've always done. I talk way too much about my guys. I'm sure I put a hex on my relationships because I just can't keep my mouth shut. But I'm learning."

"And what do you mean by that?"

"Remember I told you about Carl some time ago?"

"Yeah."

"Well, he's still around, bless his heart. I'm taking it slow and sure this time, but I think he's a keeper."

That was good news. If she didn't rush into a marriage, maybe this time it would work out. "I'm happy for you, Meredith."

"Well, I'm not happy you're going through such financial troubles. But I'm so glad you've found a great guy. My offer of help is still on the table. Any time."

"You're so sweet. But I think I can manage."

"What about Samantha?"

Oh dear. I hoped she wasn't going to make some derogatory remark now and spoil this conversation.

"She's moving with me to Jay's house." I held my breath as I awaited her reply.

She didn't say anything for a minute. Then she said, "You guys are really amazing. I wish I were as selfless as you two. But I guess my mom and dad spoiled me too much when I was a kid. It's kinda hard to get over it, you know?"

That was the first time I'd ever heard her denigrate herself. "Don't put yourself down, kiddo," I said. "Who just offered several times to help me out financially? That's as unselfish as it gets."

"I'm trying."

"Once I've gotten through the house sale and the move, maybe the four of us could get together."

"I'd love that, Liz. I miss you."

"I miss you, too," I said and realized that I meant it.

I'd told Rachel about the impending house sale, and she insisted on coming over and helping me to sort through what I wanted to move to Jay's and what I wanted to sell at a yard sale.

"You don't want to wait till the last minute to do that," she insisted. "It's going to be tough emotionally and you might as well get it over with. And maybe I can help you make the hard decisions."

So Monday morning we began to go through closets and cupboards. She'd picked up used boxes at a place on South Elm Street, and I'd begun saving newspapers a couple of weeks earlier when I realized I'd need them for packing. I'd picked up a half dozen assorted doughnuts the day before and made a pot of coffee.

I went through the kitchen cupboards holding back a minimum number of plates and glasses and silverware we would need for the next couple of weeks. The rest I handed in turn to Rachel and Samantha who wrapped them in newspaper and placed them in boxes. I found that I could get by with very little: two place settings of dinnerware and utensils, a skillet, sauce pan, coffee maker, and a few other things. I realized that I'd accumulated so much kitchenware over the years that I rarely or never used but that simply took up space. So we labeled a couple of boxes "yard sale" and quickly filled them with items I hadn't used in years.

"Do you realize you have four corkscrews?" Rachel laughed. "Someone might think you're a lush."

"I think they were all given to me as gifts. What about this Bundt cake pan? I haven't used that in decades." It was a ring-shaped pan that had been popular years before. "And the bread machine? Everyone had to have one when they came out. Now I doubt you can even get mixes for it."

"Everybody eats out now," Rachel said. "Or if they eat at home it has to be take-out or something you stick in the microwave for a couple of minutes."

"My mom had one of those," Samantha said as she placed the bread machine in the yard sale box. That was the first time she'd mentioned her mother since our discussion about her family right after she moved in with me. "I loved the sourdough bread."

"Me too," I said. "But no one seems to make it any more."

We took a doughnut and coffee break and then went to my bedroom closet. It was simple to pack all my out-of-season clothes. It was a little harder to pare down what I was wearing now, but I knew that closet and storage space would be minimal at Jay's. Samantha had come to my house with so little that her clothes would be no problem.

Next we came to my stash of art supplies.

"I just can't put these away right now," I said. "Painting is what keeps me sane."

"It shouldn't be too hard to pack them at the last minute," Rachel said. "How about if we go through the house and see what other things we can store."

We packed up boxes of books and all the decorative items that gave the house its personality. Once stripped of pictures, the Seagrove pottery, the items picked up in our travels, and rows of colorful book jackets, the rooms seemed to lose their charm. Perhaps it was good that we were doing this early. Living in a nearly barren house gave me the opportunity to wean myself of my attachment to it. It wasn't the same once it had been divested of all the beloved accessories that had given it life.

We were all pretty exhausted by late afternoon. The three of us sprawled in living room chairs after our marathon session.

"So when are you going to have your yard sale?" Rachel asked.

"Oh lord, Rachel, I'm too tired to think about it right now." Every muscle in my body ached.

"If you'll do it Saturday, I'll help you."

"Slave driver! All kidding aside, I need to get it done. I don't know what I'd do without you."

"I can help too," Samantha said. She'd done yeoman work with the packing, and I wasn't sure I'd properly acknowledged that.

"I knew you would," I said. "You've been a terrific help today."

Her face glowed with pride.

On Thursday night after class I told Jay about our packing session. We were sitting in Café Europa. Only this time I ordered a glass of wine instead of coffee. I figured I deserved it. I'd walked to class because the weather was lovely so I didn't have to worry about driving. Jay had coffee since he had to drive home.

"Why don't we take the boxes to my house this weekend and get them out of your way. Then we won't have so much to do when you move in."

"I could do it Sunday. We're having a yard sale Saturday."

"I'd like to help out but I promised Brian I'd help him work on his motorcycle. I know I shouldn't give in to his demands to appease him, but if we only have a few more months before he enlists, I want to keep our relationship as smooth as possible. Will Samantha be coming for lessons?"

"I doubt it. I don't know how long the yard sale will last."

"Then let's plan on one o'clock Sunday afternoon. We'll load up the truck then. Maybe I can enlist Brian to help me carry the boxes up to the garage storage area."

"Well, don't push him to do it. I can carry up the lighter boxes. I don't want him to resent me any more than he already does." After I said it, I realized I shouldn't have. No point in making an issue out of Brian's attitude.

Jay looked stricken. "He doesn't resent you."

"Come on, Jay. Let's get real. I know he wants your full attention. After losing his mom, that's a pretty normal reaction. I'm not hurt by it." Even as I said it I knew it wasn't true, but I didn't want Jay to be upset. I hoped time and maturity would make a difference with his son.

Jay cupped my cheek with his hand and gave me a solemn look. "You're much too generous. But that's what I love about you."

# CHAPTER TWENTY-NINE

Katherine called me the next day to say the closing on the sale of the house was scheduled for the twenty-eighth of June. That gave me a couple more weeks to finish packing up and cleaning it out. The fact that I now had a firm date brought on the strongest wave of panic yet. Before now it had seemed more like a bad dream than reality.

I placed an ad in the paper for the garage sale the next day, made a sign for the yard, and went through the boxes we'd set aside for the sale to put price tags on everything. Not being one of those bargain hunters who spend weekends going to yard sales, I had a lot of trouble deciding how much I should ask for each item. But Rachel had warned me to price everything low, otherwise nothing would sell. I'd added some things I'd found since our marathon packing session and went through the garage where Peter's tools were kept. Everything there would be sold along with the yard equipment like the mower and trimmer, hoses and shovels. I'd offered all the tools to Jay, but he already had all he needed.

Rachel came at seven Saturday morning, and the three of us set up two folding tables and carried out the boxes we'd packed on Monday. We hadn't even put everything out when buyers began to pull up out front.

"What is this?" I asked Rachel. "My ad said the sale starts at eight o'clock, and it's not much after seven thirty. What are these people doing here?"

"The dealers always get to the sales first. The ones who have stores or booths at big flea markets check out all the yard sales for bargains. People often don't know how to price things, and they can pick up real deals from unsuspecting sellers."

"Well, you're the one who told me to make everything cheap. Am I giving anything away here?"

Two women were closely perusing the items closest to the curb, picking things up and examining them and putting them down again.

Rachel hurriedly looked over the knickknacks on the table near us. "No, I think you've packed away everything that was valuable. This is just typical yard sale stuff."

I laughed and punched her on the arm. "Are you making derogatory remarks about my beautiful treasures?"

"Well, you know how it is—one man's trash is another man's treasure. Maybe they'll think this stuff is priceless."

"Priceless meaning it ain't worth a thing."

Rachel shrugged. "You said it; I didn't."

We kept up our banter the rest of the morning to stave off the blues. Samantha was manning the cash box, and she'd look at us occasionally as though we'd lost our minds. I wasn't sure Samantha had ever developed a funny bone. She looked at us skeptically when Rachel and I teased each other, apparently wondering whether we were serious or not. But I suppose there hadn't been much room for hilarity in her life. And right now my own laughter was hiding a lot of pain.

By noon the tables were virtually empty. A few items were left but only an occasional shopper came by, and most left without buying anything.

"What say we pack up what's left and take it to the thrift store," I said.

The three of us stowed what was left over in one of the boxes we'd brought out to the lawn.

"Let me fix us a bite of lunch before we go," I said folding in the top flaps when the box was full.

"I'll help," Samantha said.

"Me, too," chimed in Rachel.

We hauled the box to my car and put it in the back, folded up the tables which Jay had said he could use and took them back to the house. We fixed toasted cheese sandwiches and tomato soup and sat down to eat. It reminded me of when I had fixed it with Jay.

The doorbell rang as I finished my last spoonful of soup. I wondered if a late yard sale shopper was checking to see if anything was left. They should know that by twelve thirty everything would be gone.

Jay was standing on my porch grinning when I opened the door. "Don't tell me it's over," he said.

"What are you doing here? Come on in," I waved him into the room. "I thought you were helping Brian with his bike."

He gave me a hello kiss. "The problem wasn't as serious as he thought. We got done in record time."

"We're having lunch. Want a toasted cheese sandwich? I'm afraid the soup is gone." We'd split my last two cans of tomato soup between us.

"That sounds good. How'd the sale go?"

"Not bad. We had a few things left over, but we packed them up to take to the thrift store."

"How about after we eat, we load the boxes you're going to keep at my place in my truck. Then we'll drive by the store on Battleground Avenue to drop off what you have for them, and you and Samantha can follow me up to Summerfield. We'll store your things over the garage and maybe have time for a lesson for Samantha."

"You sure?"

"Of course."

"Come on back to the kitchen. Maybe I can find more than a cheese sandwich for you. You'll need sustenance if you're going to lift those boxes."

Jay greeted Rachel and Samantha who'd finished their meals by now. Both seemed very pleased to see him. He had a way of bringing sunshine and energy into a room.

The three of them sat around the table and talked while I made a couple of sandwiches for him and found a can of bean with bacon soup at the back of the cupboard.

Jay questioned Rachel about her writing, and she told him she'd started a novel. "I'd always thought it would be too daunting to write a whole book," she said, "but I decided to think of the chapters as a series of short stories and that made it more manageable."

I stood stirring the soup as it warmed and felt a pang of guilt. I'd been so wrapped up in my own problems I hadn't even asked Rachel about her writing lately. I'd become way too self-involved. "How far along are you, Rachel?" I asked.

"It's hard to tell. I tried to outline it before I started writing, but I found I just couldn't do that. I'm kind of going along blindly, letting it take me where it may. So I don't know how long it will be in the end. But I'm about a hundred pages into it."

"Do you have an agent?" Jay asked. He seemed to know more about publishing than I did.

"One got in touch with me when he saw my story in *Glimmer Train* and asked if I had anything in the works. I told him I'd just begun a novel, and he asked to see it when it was done."

"That's fantastic!" I exclaimed. "Why didn't you tell me that, Rachel?"

She was holding her glass of tea with both hands, twisting it back and forth on the table top and looking uncomfortable. "You've been going through so much, Liz. I thought it would be cruel to tell you about my good luck. Besides, he might hate it. Just because he wants to see it doesn't mean he'll take me on."

"Nonsense," Jay said. "You write like a dream, Rachel. I'll bet he'll love it." I hadn't realized that Jay had read Rachel's short stories. I felt mortified to think I'd never asked to read them. What kind of friend was I?

"Can I have a lesson at your house today?" Samantha piped up. She'd barely said a word since Jay arrived. She always seemed afraid that she was butting in on other people's conversations. But Jay put her at ease.

"Sure. After we get the boxes stored away in the garage. It might be shorter than usual, but we'll do something."

After Jay finished eating, we began carrying the cartons from my bedroom out to his truck. I suggested to Samantha that she clean up the kitchen while the rest of us carried them down the steps and stacked them in the back of the pickup. She was still doing therapy on her own for her leg, and I didn't want to take a chance that she would fall on the front steps and reinjure it. She'd asked me once if I thought she could go back to her job at the assisted living facility. I'd told her it was too soon, that she needed to heal more, but truthfully I didn't want her to have to go back there. What I'd hoped would happen was that she could enroll at Guilford Tech in the fall. But she'd need a full scholarship for that now. I'd try to see what I could do about that after we'd settled in at Jay's.

Once the truck was loaded and Rachel had left, Jay led the way across Wendover Avenue to Battleground to the thrift store near Horse Pen Creek Road. Jay pulled through the drop off line and parked and came back to unload my car. Then we got back on the road to Summerfield. I thought I'd better get used to this drive since I was going to be making it a lot come July.

# CHAPTER THIRTY

As we drove up the highway which had now become two-lane Route 220, I thought what a lovely drive it was. Deep woods lined the road for miles with side streets leading into unseen upscale neighborhoods. The Center for Creative Leadership where executives came from all over the country for leadership training could be seen amidst the trees just north of town. The road eventually crossed a low earthen dam between Lake Higgins and Lake Brandt before coming upon the small shopping areas that mark the southern edge of Summerfield. It is in this area that we took a side road to Jay's place.

Horse farms and pastures bordered the roads punctuated by wooded lots. Within ten minutes we approached Jay's drive. His house, set well back from the road, couldn't be seen until you'd driven partway down the driveway.

As I followed Jay down the drive, I spotted a car parked in front of the house. It wasn't until we got closer that I realized it was a sheriff's car.

Oh no, I thought, is Brian in trouble again? Jay had so hoped that his son had turned his life around. How would Jay react if he was in custody? The beautiful day had instantly been transformed into one of foreboding.

"How come there's a police car here?" Samantha asked as we approached.

"I have no idea," I said. "Let's hope it isn't something bad."

Jay pulled up beside the sheriff's car as two deputies got out.

There was no sign of Brian. I'd thought perhaps he'd be in the back seat, but the car was empty.

Jay got out and walked over to them as I parked behind him and jumped out of my car to join them. Samantha stayed in her seat.

"Mr. Kadlacek?" the taller man asked. He had graying hair and a little paunch. The other one was much younger and slimmer. Both of the men looked grim.

"That's me," Jay said. I could tell how tense he was as a muscle in his jaw was twitching, and I detected a slight tremor in his hands that hung by his side.

"Are you related to Brian Kadlacek?"

Oh god, I knew it. Brian had gone off the rail.

"I'm his father," said Jay who looked like he was about to explode.

"I'm sorry. I'm afraid I have some bad news for you," the deputy said.

Jay couldn't seem to speak; he just looked at the deputy with an expression of unmitigated dread.

"There's been an accident. Brian lost control of his motorcycle on Route 158 and slammed into a tree."

"He's . . . he's . . . how bad is it?" Jay finally stammered. He put his hand on the roof of the sheriff's car to steady himself.

"They've taken him to Moses Cone. He's in pretty bad shape."

Jay covered his face with his hands in stunned disbelief. Finally he looked at the deputy and said, "I'm on my way. Thanks for coming here to tell me. I appreciate it."

"We thought you'd want to know as soon as possible, and since we were in the area we decided to see if you were home rather than call you. We've just been here a few minutes." The men got in their sheriff's car and drove away.

Jay turned to me. "Will you come with me? And Samantha

too, of course."

"Absolutely."

"Then we need to take your car. Can't get three in the truck."

I handed him the keys and he jumped into the driver's seat. Samantha was in front so I got into the back.

As we peeled out of the driveway I said, "Don't have an accident yourself trying to get there."

He let up slightly on the gas but still drove over the speed limit as he headed back to 220.

We made it to the hospital in about twenty minutes as Jay wove in and out of traffic with an urgency that I well understood.

He stopped in front of the emergency room entrance and hopped out and ran inside. I told him I'd find a parking space and we'd join him shortly. That was before I realized I had to park at the farthest edge in the crowded lot. Samantha couldn't walk very fast and I didn't want to sprint ahead and leave her, so it took us ten minutes to return.

Jay had disappeared, and I assumed he was with Brian. I asked at the reception area and was told only family members were allowed with the patient. So Samantha and I settled into the waiting area. She picked up a magazine, but I was much too nervous to read. A TV set was droning away on CNN, but I didn't try to watch. It was usually bad news, and I couldn't take any more than I already had.

It was nearly an hour before Jay appeared in the waiting room. His face was drained of color, and he looked on the verge of collapse. He stood for a moment in the doorway staring into space. It was obvious he didn't see me; I wondered what awful vision he saw and if it was realistic or his imagination was taking him to the darkest possible places.

I jumped up and ran to him. Taking his hand I led him back to where we sat, and he slumped into the chair between us.

"How is he, Jay?" I asked, taking his hands in mine. Was

Brian dead? If he was, I didn't know if Jay could deal with it. It hadn't been long since his wife died, and he'd agonized over the problems with his son. He'd tried so hard to heal their relationship, but Brian still had a chip on his shoulder. Would Jay somehow blame himself for this?

He looked at me, his eyes bloodshot and grief written across his features. "He has severe head injuries. They're going to have to operate to alleviate the pressure on the brain. He's in a coma. What are we going to do?" And he broke down and buried his face in his hands.

Samantha, looking on in horror, fished in her pocketbook and brought out a little packet of tissues. "Here, Jay," she said handing it to him.

He took it from her, patting her hand. "Thanks, Sam." He'd never called her that before, but it sounded like an endearment.

Neither of us spoke but let him regain his composure. He was leaning forward, his face cupped in his hands as he silently cried. It broke my heart to watch him.

Finally he wiped his eyes with one of Sam's tissues and sat back. "They'll be taking him to surgery soon. I'm sure I'll be here the rest of the night. You two go on home now, and I'll call you tomorrow when I need a ride."

"I'm not leaving you, Jay. I'm staying as long as you are." I looked across him at Samantha. "Okay with you? I can call a cab if you want to go home."

"No, please, I want to stay too."

"Okay then. I'm afraid you're stuck with us."

He gave us a wan smile and nodded.

It was late afternoon when they told Jay they were taking Brian to the operating room. They told us where the surgical waiting room was on an upper floor.

"Let me go bring back some take out for you to eat," I said.

Jay shook his head. "I'm not hungry. But you guys go get a

bite. I know it's going to be a while before we hear anything."

I knew it was useless to argue with him, so Samantha and I went to a drive-in restaurant on Summit Avenue, hoping I'd find a parking space when I returned. That seemed more appealing than hospital cafeteria food, and in spite of what he said, I planned to take something back to Jay. He needed to keep his strength up because he had a long and difficult road ahead of him.

We each had cheeseburgers, tater tots and slushes, comfort food if you will, and I ordered the same for Jay except I got him a cup of coffee. He, unlike me, could drink caffeine at all hours without it interfering with his sleep. Even if it did, I knew he would want to stay awake this evening.

Miraculously, I found a parking space nearer the building when we returned, and we wound our way through hospital corridors to the waiting room.

Jay sat staring at the floor, arms resting on knees, massaging his forehead with his fingertips.

"Here. Eat," I said in my most commanding voice as I thrust the sack of food at him.

He looked up. "I'm not hungry."

"Eat anyway."

He took the bag and set it on his lap without opening it.

"Jay," I said, "do it for me."

Finally he opened it and ate half the burger and a third of the tater tots. "I can't eat another bite," he said. Since he made the effort I didn't urge him again. He did drink the coffee.

We sat for the next couple of hours in almost total silence. I tried to look at the weeks-old magazines that were strewn about, but not a thing I read registered. Samantha found a book of word puzzles that she worked on but Jay could do nothing but sit and deal with his ominous speculations.

At last, near midnight, the surgeon came out and asked for Jay.

"Brian is doing as well as can be expected," he said. "He was in a coma when he came in, and we'll have to keep him in a medically-induced coma for some days while the brain is swelling. The chances are good he'll survive, but I have to be honest with you; I don't know how much brain damage there is. We'll just have to wait and see."

"When can I see him?" Jay pleaded.

"It'll be a while yet. He's in the recovery room and will be taken to ICU. As soon as he is settled in we'll let you know."

Wrapped in a cocoon of fear and grief, the three of us spent the next several hours in the waiting room as visions of the unthinkable haunted our thoughts.

# CHAPTER THIRTY-ONE

Samantha and I finally curled up on sofas and fell asleep for a while, but Jay maintained his vigil. It was early morning before they allowed him to visit Brian. He was gone only thirty minutes before returning.

"How is he?" I said, jumping up to greet him.

"It's hard to tell. He has so many monitors and tubes and a trach that it's almost grotesque. But he seems to be hanging in there. I'm only allowed to see him for a few minutes every few hours. So let's go home so we all can catch a little shut eye."

This time I drove because Jay was too tired and I had caught a little sleep. By the time I dropped him off at his house it was five A.M.

"Can I go with you when you go back to visit him?" I asked.

"Only family members are supposed to be in ICU," he said. "There isn't much point, anyway, since he's not awake."

"Look, Jay," I said, suddenly coming up with the idea, "why don't you plan to stay with me as long as he's in ICU. No sense in driving all the way back and forth to Summerfield."

"But you don't have room."

"I've got an air mattress that I can put in my bedroom for me and Sam can sleep in my bed. You can have the guest room."

"No way," Samantha said. "I'll sleep on the air mattress. You keep your bed."

"Okay then. Why don't you pack a bag, Jay, and come on back to my house?"

Jay managed a smile. "You ladies are the best. Tell you what—
let me get a few hours' sleep, unload the boxes from the back of
the truck, and then I'll drive on down." He climbed wearily out
of the passenger seat and looked as though he might drop before
he even got in the house.

"We'll expect you for lunch then," I told him. He blew us a
kiss, and we watched as he unlocked his door and went inside.

Jay stayed with me for the next two weeks until the day I had
the closing on the house. He went to visit Brian in ICU every
few hours. In the meantime the three of us took what furniture
we could to store over his garage.

When he first suggested that we go ahead and move what we
could, I'd asked him the question I'd been avoiding.

"I've been thinking about that, Jay. When Brian is able to
come home, you're not going to want us there, too. You'll have
enough on your hands without two women in your hair." I had
no idea where I *could* go, but I wanted him to know that he was
off the hook as far as the two of us were concerned.

"Nonsense," he said. "Until he's well, I'll probably have a
hospital bed in the living room to make it easier to care for him.
If you can put up with that, I very much want you to stay with
me. In fact, you can lend me your moral support. I'm going to
need it."

I wondered if Brian was ever going to get well. But if Jay felt
we could help in some way that was good enough for me.

By the time the day came to sign the papers on the house,
not much had changed with Brian's condition. The swelling had
gone down in his brain and the doctors were no longer induc-
ing a coma, but he had yet to wake up. Jay had taken the position that he would awaken and that eventually he'd be back to
normal. I applauded him for his positive outlook, but I found it
impossible to share it, though I never said so.

I went to the closing while Jay went to the hospital. We planned to move out the remaining furniture the following day. He had arranged to rent a U-Haul truck and had enlisted the help of a couple of his friends to load it.

I finally met the husband and wife who bought my house at the lawyer's office. A young couple who were buying their first home, they seemed thrilled at the prospect of living there. It made me feel better to know the new owners loved it and would take good care of it. It was a bittersweet moment, but Brian's accident made me realize how much worse things can be than what I was going through.

The next morning, Earl Bernard, the painter from Sternberger, knocked on my door. It was so good to see him again.

"Liz, how are you?" he asked gathering me in a bear hug. "We miss you over at the artists' center."

"I miss being there." He had no idea how much I yearned for that lovely studio.

"Well, you couldn't be moving in with a nicer guy. What a shame about his son though."

"It is. It's tragic."

"I know how much he looks forward to having you stay with him. He shouldn't be alone."

"I hope it'll help. Well, don't just stand there, come on in." I opened the door wide and shooed him into the living room.

I introduced him to Samantha who was packing up the last of the dishware and glasses.

"Jay tells me you're quite a good painter," he told her.

She broke out in one of her rare smiles. "He said that?"

"Absolutely."

I knew that made her day.

Jay pulled up in the U-Haul truck just then. A stranger got out with him, and he introduced him. Kyle Blanchard taught pottery at the art center.

Between the three of them it didn't take long to carry the remaining furniture out to the truck. I ordered four large pizzas to be delivered which we ate hungrily once the house was empty.

Kyle and Earl climbed in Earl's car, and Samantha and I hopped in mine, and we all followed Jay in the rental truck. As I pulled out of my driveway, I took one long last look at my former home. It was hard to explain, but I didn't have a twinge of regret. I'd had some great times there and wouldn't forget it. But I'd worked past it by now and was feeling only relief that it had sold and I was on my way to a new life.

Samantha looked out the window and said wistfully, "Goodbye house. I liked you a lot. I hope I like my next place, too."

It didn't take but an hour for the three men to cart the contents of the truck up to the attic over the garage. They all exchanged high fives when the job was done, and Samantha, Jay and I collapsed in his living room.

It wasn't long, though, before Jay looked at his watch and said, "Gotta go see Brian."

"I'll check out your cupboards and see what I can put together for supper," I said.

"Make a list of what you need, and we'll go grocery shopping tomorrow."

He left and Samantha and I checked out the bedroom that Jay had made available for us. It was simply furnished but comfortable enough. We both had packed suitcases with our clothes, and we hung them in our shared closet. It was small, as closets always are in older houses, but we hung up what we could and stored the rest in the dresser. Samantha's wardrobe was very small, so she took up little space. I'd planned on buying her new clothes for school or a decent job before the bottom fell out of my finances, but I could no longer do that.

After rummaging through his kitchen, I was able to cobble together a meal of fried chicken breasts, instant mashed potatoes, and canned green beans when Jay got home. He said there was no change in Brian's condition.

"This is great," gushed Jay as he ate, although I thought the dinner was pretty pathetic. I didn't know if he was trying to make me feel good or was relishing the fact that someone was cooking for him. Sometimes a mediocre meal can become special from the mere fact you don't have to fix it.

We were all dead tired and ready to go to bed by nine. Samantha went upstairs ahead of us.

"I'm glad you're here," Jay said solemnly after she'd left. "The nights alone have been the worst. I can't get Brian out of my mind."

I nodded. "I remember when Peter was sick. It seemed sometimes like the nights would never end."

He looked at me intently. "I want to ask you something, Liz."

"Fire away."

"I want you in my bedroom. Not the guest room." He looked at me with longing.

I didn't say anything, trying to get my conflicting emotions under control.

"Please." His eyes were sad and pleading which made him irresistible.

We hadn't been intimate since Brian was hurt. Actually it had been longer than that because the opportunity hadn't presented itself. But now that I was living with Jay, I needed to decide if I could make that commitment. Once done, it would be hard to undo. But I loved this man so much.

"Yes, Jay, I will. I do love you, you know." It was the first time I dared to say that to him.

He sat down beside me on the couch and enfolded me in his arms. He kissed me long and tenderly. His lips felt so right on mine. Then he held me at arms' length and looked at me with great seriousness. "I want to marry you, Liz. Will you be my wife?"

This took me totally by surprise. He'd never mentioned matrimony before. For some reason I'd gotten the impression that he never planned to marry again. But I was willing to be with him anyway, although I'd never thought in a million years that I could live with a man out of wedlock. But people change, *I'd* changed, and I didn't want to lose him. He was too special, too fine a man.

I wrapped my arms around his neck and said, "I can't think of anything I'd rather do than become your wife."

After another tender kiss he said, "I want to wait until Brian can attend the ceremony. That could take weeks or months. Is that okay with you?"

I could understand why he wanted Brian to be included. If we went ahead while he was recovering and presented it as a surprise, it would be devastating for him. "As long as he can't veto it. I know he isn't crazy about the idea of me being with you."

"Look, Liz, I'm not going to let him rule my life any more. He may need a lot of physical help when he gets home, and I'm willing to give him that. He can no longer hold sway over my emotions. And I don't want you to think I'm doing this because I'll need someone to take care of him. I plan to hire help for that. I would never expect you to take on that burden."

"As long as we are talking about responsibilities, I still feel responsible for Samantha. She's not quite ready to be on her own yet."

"That works for me."

We sat quietly and simply smiled at each other for the next several minutes. We'd had so much drama in our lives, we rejoiced in this quiet happy moment.

Finally he took my hand and led me up to *our* bed.

219

# CHAPTER THIRTY-TWO

Jay continued to teach his classes and work visits to the hospital in between. I accompanied him to Thursday night classes and spent some time painting in his studio. Luckily the building was large and accommodated all three of us because Samantha was painting in earnest now every day. I rarely went to the hospital because Brian was still in a coma and there was nothing I could do.

I spent a lot of time job hunting. With help from Jay, I learned how to find job opportunities on line, and I sent out dozens of resumes in response to those I thought might fit me. Unfortunately my resume was not impressive, my only job having been in the office of the jewelry store. I didn't have the advanced computer skills needed for so many jobs today. The other thing against me was my age, although I tried not to make it obvious I was in my mid-fifties. I knew, though, if I ever got an interview I couldn't pass for a twenty-something, not even a forty-something. But that seemed to be a moot point at the moment since I got absolutely no response.

Instead I tried to brighten up Jay's home with some of the things I'd brought with me. A bare light bulb hung in the space above the garage which gave me enough light to go through my boxes looking for anything that might make it more homey. Jay didn't object at all; in fact he seemed pleased with the changes I made. I didn't buy anything new, but I created pillow covers and curtains from colorful linens on my sewing machine.

Around the living room I placed some of the mementoes I'd collected on trips and repainted walls that had become dingy. In no time the house looked a lot more like a home.

The weather had become hot and muggy. The house had no central air conditioning, but Jay had installed window units in almost every room as well as in the studio. Samantha and I spent much of our days painting now. She seemed to thrive as her art became more proficient. It was as if at last she had something she could be proud of.

One evening after dinner while we were still seated at the table Jay said, "Sam, I have a request to make."

She looked a little startled. "Like what?"

"I'd like you to pose for me. I want to paint your picture."

With a look of distress, she cupped her cheeks with her hands as if trying to hide her face. "Oh, no. You don't want to do that."

He smiled at her in his kind way. "Of course I do. I wouldn't have asked you otherwise."

Her face reddened. "But I'm so ugly."

It broke my heart. Her low self-esteem had been reinforced over the years until it had crippled her emotionally.

Jay reached across the small table and touched her arm, and she flinched. I'd learned long ago that she avoided contact with others. When she first came to live with me, I'd tried on occasion to hug her, but she always seemed so uncomfortable I'd given up on physical contact.

I could tell Jay was taken aback by her reaction, but he soldiered on. "You're not ugly, Sam. You're unique. You have your own special kind of beauty. And that's what I want to prove to you. Let me paint you. I'll give you the painting, and you can do whatever you want with it—throw it away or hang it in your room or whatever. Would you do that for me?"

She frowned as if she couldn't believe what he was saying. She sat silently for a couple of minutes chewing on her lip lost in thought. Finally she said, "Well, I guess so. If you promise not to show it to anyone else."

"You can decide that after it's done. How about tomorrow night?"

She sighed. "Okay."

The next morning at breakfast Jay said, "Don't forget, Sam. Tonight's the night."

She made a face but said nothing.

After he left we cleared off the dishes. I washed as Samantha dried.

"Would you like for me to put some curlers in your hair?" I asked. Her hair was stick straight and she always pulled it back in a ponytail. "How about I fluff it up a little for your portrait?"

"Like you think it's going to make a difference?" she said. She wouldn't look me in the eye but dried the dish she was holding till she practically rubbed the design off it.

"Everybody needs a little perking up when they have their picture taken. I've always gone to the hairdresser before I've had my photo taken. Since we can't afford a hairdresser, I think I can do a fair job at least."

She shrugged noncommittally. "Whatever."

I hoped that Jay knew what he was doing when he'd suggested this. But I wondered if it might backfire. If she hated it, what then?

That afternoon she let me shampoo her hair and roll it up in curlers after I'd cut off a few inches. She'd always cut her own hair standing at the bathroom sink and whacking away at it with my sewing scissors. She didn't care whether it was even or not.

I was anything but expert at fixing hair but I thought a little softness around her face wouldn't hurt.

Together we went through her wardrobe to decide what she

would wear. Her clothes consisted mainly of tee shirts and jeans, but there was one white blouse with a collar that I'd bought for her when she went job hunting and some black slacks.

When Jay came home, Samantha was dressed in the blouse and slacks, and I'd combed out her hair. I was surprised at how good it looked. The waves around her face covered the misshapen ears and softened her features. Of course Samantha would never be pretty, but she looked better than I'd ever seen.

"Wow!" Jay enthused, "Sam, you look great!"

I wanted to kiss him right then and there.

Her face reddened, and she smiled shyly. "Liz fixed my hair."

"Well, maybe she's missed her calling. You need to have her fix it for you more often."

She looked at me questioningly.

"Of course I will," I said.

After dinner we all went out to the studio, and Jay posed Samantha on a chair on the little podium. He hadn't asked any models to come to his house since we moved in, preferring to paint them at the arts center. We'd decided having nude models might not be the best thing with Samantha living there. He didn't want her to be uncomfortable. He had only used models when Brian was in school, but Samantha was there all day.

I sat beside him as he sketched her on the canvas and began to paint. I'd never watched him from beginning to end of a painting, and I found it very instructive. His movements were so sure and swift, unlike my tentative strokes. He put in a mid-toned layer of burnt sienna and cobalt blue over the entire canvas and, when it dried, blocked in the whole composition with burnt sienna. He began with the darkest darks and painted the deep shadow areas. Mixing alizarin crimson, sap green, and titanium white he put in the shadowed skin tones and then he began to lay in the light skin tones with a mixture of cadmium red light, Indian yellow and titanium white. It wasn't long before a likeness of Samantha began to emerge.

He worked about two hours and then, sensing that Samantha was tiring, claimed he was done for the evening.

"Can I see it?" Samantha asked as she stretched her tired muscles.

"Not till it's done," Jay said. He picked up the canvas and carried it to the back room where he stored it.

As we walked back to the house, Samantha and I trailed Jay.

"What does it look like?" she whispered to me when she was sure he was out of earshot.

"It looks like a very basic beginning of a portrait. You really can't tell anything at this stage."

"Darn," she said.

I had hopes that her eagerness to see it signaled a change in attitude and she was happy about it. I prayed that she would be pleased with the results. Otherwise everyone was going to be disappointed.

Jay worked on the portrait for the next several evenings. Samantha sat patiently without complaint. I watched as he almost magically constructed a likeness of her that was very recognizable but at the same time enhanced her best features and minimized the anomalies due to the Noonan Syndrome. I thought it was masterful.

Finally he said, "Okay, Sam, come and see."

She walked very tentatively over to us, and I could tell she was at once eager to have a chance to see it and frightened to encounter her own likeness preserved in such a timeless manner.

Jay stood back, and she walked around the easel. She stood staring at it for several minutes in silence. My heart was in my throat anticipating her reaction.

Finally she turned around and looked up at Jay. A slow smile filled her face. "I like it, Jay. I like it a lot."

His face lit up too. "See I told you you're prettier than you know. I hope you want to keep it."

"I do. I do. I want to hang it in my bedroom."

"As soon as it dries I'll give it a coat of varnish and frame it for you. Then we'll get it hung up on your wall."

Samantha took two steps and threw her arms around Jay in a hug. Over her head he looked at me in astonishment. I was equally surprised; she never showed spontaneous affection that way. I gave him two thumbs up.

# CHAPTER THIRTY-THREE

The last week of July, Jay called me from the hospital in the middle of the afternoon. "Brian's awake!" he exclaimed. "He seemed to recognize me. But he hasn't spoken yet."

"Oh, that's wonderful," I said. "Have you talked to the doctor?"

"No, I've got the word out that I want to see him. So don't wait dinner for me. I don't know how long I'll be here."

I passed the word along to Samantha.

"I'm so glad for them," she said. Ever since Jay had painted her portrait, her admiration of him was obvious. That act of kindness had washed away any remnants of doubt about him.

I kept dinner warm for Jay—you can't do much to hurt meat loaf—and I planned to whip up instant mashed potatoes and cook some frozen peas when he came home, a typical meal I threw together in my present funk. Brian's condition brought an aura of gloom to all of us, no matter how hard we tried to dispel it. Every day we waited for the change that didn't happen. But today's news was a baby step toward normalcy. I vowed I'd put together a gourmet meal the next night in celebration.

It was almost nine before Jay got home. As he ate his dinner, he told us about his conversation with the doctor.

"Brian's got a very long way to go. In fact no one knows how much he'll improve. It's good he's awake now but he's going to have to relearn how to do everything: walk, talk, feed himself. The doctor recommended that he go to the Shepherd Center.

226

It's a rehab facility in Atlanta that specializes in brain injuries. Some people make complete recoveries there, but there's no guarantee, of course." Jay picked at his food, wavering between hope and despair.

But I was relieved that at least there was a chance of recovery. It sounded like a long tough road. "How will he get there?"

"They're arranging a med evac flight. They want him to go as soon as possible."

"Can you go with him?"

"Yeah. I'll go down and make the arrangements and catch a commercial flight home." His voice was so tired. He knew that in spite of Brian's improvement, there wasn't cause for celebration yet.

"Isn't there some way you can stay down there with him?" It would be traumatic for both of them for Jay to leave when Brian was in such bad shape.

"I've got to teach and paint, Liz. I need the income. I'll try to drive down once a month to see him."

Samantha had been silent up till now. "I have something I'd like to give Brian for his room. Could you take it with you?"

"I don't know, Sam. There won't be a lot of space in my carry on. How big is it?"

"I'll go get it," she said and went upstairs.

She came back carrying a 9″ × 12″ sketchbook. She opened it and handed it to Jay. I peeked over his shoulder as he opened it and looked at the page she had marked. It was a watercolor of a meadow filled with wildflowers with low hills in the background. The sky was partially dark but the scene was lit up by a rainbow arching over the page. She'd done a remarkable job of rendering a difficult subject. The rainbow could have been garish and looked like a grade school effort, but she'd made it wispy and ethereal and beautiful. The message was clear.

"I was going to give it to him when he came home, but he

might like it for his room down there. Maybe it will cheer him up."

"Good job," Jay said smiling up at her. "I'll find a frame for it and pack it in my overnight bag. I know Brian will appreciate it."

Two days later Jay left to accompany Brian to Atlanta. He intended to spend two nights there before returning home.

I called Rachel and invited her to come for lunch the next day. She and I hadn't seen each other since the day of the garage sale. I'd given up serving meals at Urban Ministry in the turmoil surrounding the sale of my house and the subsequent move, and Rachel had asked a neighbor to go with her. She'd told me they had all the help they needed at this time, but she'd let me know if a vacancy occurred. I was beginning to feel that I wasn't much use to anyone.

But I was anxious to see her. I'd fixed chicken salad and fresh fruit and made brownies for dessert.

She and I greeted each other like long lost sisters. I hadn't realized how much I missed her. She took Samantha's hand—surprisingly she didn't withdraw it—and said, "You look great, Samantha. Love your hair."

"Liz fixed it for me." She patted her head with pride.

"Maybe you ought to consider going professional," Rachel said to me. I don't think she was serious but meant it as a compliment. Since I hadn't been able to find a job I wondered if I should consider going to beauty school. But the idea of standing on my feet all day discouraged me.

"And what's new with you?" I asked.

"It looks like I have an agent. At his urging I sent him a partial manuscript for my novel, and he loved it. I'm over the moon, Liz." She was so fired up I thought she was going to bounce out of her chair. She'd always been animated, but now she almost vibrated with excitement.

"You're on your way, girl," I said. I couldn't have been happier for her.

I didn't want to spoil her euphoric mood, but when she asked me what was going on in my life I told her about my unproductive job hunt and how discouraging it was.

"I just heard that the United Arts Council will have an opening. The gal that oversees Sternberger Arts Center is leaving because her husband was transferred. That would be perfect for you."

"Oh, Rachel, I could kiss you. Not that I have much of a chance, but I'll go down there tomorrow. Jay's flight gets in at three something, but I'd have plenty of time to check it out in the morning."

"You've got as much chance as anyone. More, because of the time you spent at Sternberger."

I purposely refused to contemplate my chances at getting the job. It would be perfect as far as I was concerned, but I was afraid to want it too much.

We spent the afternoon chatting about nothing in particular. Samantha had excused herself to go to the studio to paint. I told Rachel about her growing talent.

"Not that I've seen that much of her," Rachel said, "but it seems to me she's blossomed. She contributes more to the conversation and generally seems happier."

"I give Jay a lot of credit for that," I said. "He's made her feel very welcome here."

"Don't minimize your own involvement. You're really bringing out the best in her." Rachel took a sip of her ice tea that she'd brought from the kitchen. I'd always teased her that she epitomized the South's love of sweet tea. She drank it all day long.

"I try to make her feel comfortable. That's the least I can do."

"I've always admired you for taking her in. You didn't have to."

"Yes I did. I couldn't have forgiven myself if I'd left Samantha to wither away in a homeless shelter." But that didn't mean I never wished it had been different. Though I'd never admit it out loud, there were days when I deeply resented the fact that Peter had put me in this position. And though I tried hard not to feel angry, my memory of him had been diminished by the revelation of his illegitimate daughter.

All I could say was thank god Jay accepted her as part of the family. I don't know how I could have handled his rejection of her.

# CHAPTER THIRTY-FOUR

The next morning I dressed in my career woman mode and drove to the Cultural Arts Center. Since the position had not yet been vacated, I decided to take a chance on simply showing up instead of making an appointment for an interview. I was afraid if I called they would put me off until the opening was officially advertised, and I'd be up against a whole slew of applicants. I knew it was risky, but I was so desperate I was willing to take the chance.

I went directly to the office where I'd made arrangements to rent the studio at Sternberger the year before. Audrey Stone, the woman I'd talked to then, was behind a big desk piled high with file folders. The room was small and claustrophobic—it had no windows—but the walls were covered with brightly hued posters that gave it a lively appearance. There was also some original art which I suspected was donated by artists who had studios in the old house. I was excited at the possibility of working directly with them. I crossed my fingers behind my back in a childish effort to increase my chances. At this point I was willing to stand on my head if it meant my luck would improve.

"Hi," I said. "Please forgive me for interrupting your work. I'm Liz Raynor, and I had a studio at Sternberger for over a year. I had to give it up recently when I had some financial difficulty. But I have to tell you that having that studio made all the difference in my life. It is such a magical place."

Audrey smiled at me. "Sit down," she said gesturing to the

one chair in the office. "I need a break anyway. What can I do for you?"

"I saw Rachel Levine yesterday. She has the dining room studio."

"Oh, sure. Rachel's been there a long time." Audrey settled back in her tilting chair and took a sip from the coffee cup on her desk.

"She told me she'd heard you're moving out of town."

A sad look passed over Audrey's face. "Yeah. My husband has been transferred. We're moving to Connecticut. I hate leaving Greensboro, but mostly I hate leaving my job."

"I'm sorry to hear that. Maybe it will be a good change for you. Have they found a replacement yet? I need a job desperately, Audrey." I hated to sound like I was begging, I wouldn't have done it in an official interview, but I wanted her to know that I wasn't just looking for a job to fill my time, that I really needed it. "I have experience working in a jewelry store office so I know how to manage things, and since I am familiar with Sternberger, I'd be a good one to oversee it."

Audrey sat forward and put her elbows on her desk. "I'm not the one who does the hiring here."

"I understand that. Perhaps you'll put in a good word for me. Maybe I could talk to the HR director before the position is made public?" I asked her hopefully.

Audrey pondered my request as she took another swallow of coffee. "Let me suggest something. You know all the people who have studios there. I can give you their contact numbers. Why don't you ask them all to write to Connie Grayson, that's who's doing the hiring, and lobby for you. Have them tell her what a great manager you'd be. That would impress her. But do it now. She's about to post the position on line."

I jumped up and leaned over her desk to shake her hand. "Thank you so much," I said. "I'm going over there right now.

Rachel will be there at least. I'll call the others."

She turned to her computer, brought up the tenant list, and printed it out for me. "Don't tell anyone I gave you this," she said handing it to me. "I'm really not supposed to give out this information, so be discreet."

I put my hand over my heart. "On my honor . . . Thank you so much, Audrey. Good luck with your move!" I folded the paper, stuck it in my purse, and blew her a kiss.

Peeking through the glass door of the dining room at Sternberger, I could see Rachel working on a laptop when I knocked on her door.

"I can't believe you're using a computer!" I said when she let me in.

"Liz! I'm so glad to see you. I bought it with the money I got from a couple of short stories. I decided there was no way I could write an entire novel in long hand. I know there are people who do it that way, but even a short story gives me writer's cramp." She massaged her fingers as if it hurt to think about it.

"Well, welcome to the modern world." I told her about my meeting with Audrey.

"That sounds really promising. I'll write my letter immediately. Oh, I hope you get it, Liz." She gave me a hug.

I met Jay at the airport later in the afternoon. He looked tired and somber as he greeted me.

"How'd it go?" I asked after we hugged.

"It's a wonderful place. No doubt about that. It's just that Brian has such a long road ahead of him. I talked with the doctors and therapists. They couldn't give me any guarantees. But they said they'd do the best they could for him. We'll just have to wait and see."

"Could they give you any idea how long it might take?"

"Every case is different. But it will be at least a few months.

They'll let me know if it gets to the point he is no longer making progress."

I didn't want to think about that. What if he needed round-the-clock care for the rest of his life?

At the supper table he told Samantha and me more about the facility. "Shepherd Pathways has twelve beds for people who have sustained acute brain injuries. The staff works to restore all the life skills they've lost as well as vocational therapy. They have specially trained coaches who work on behavior and personal management."

He told us about some individual cases he'd heard about who'd made almost complete recoveries. "Those stories are what keep me going."

To change to a more upbeat subject I told them about my visit to the United Arts Council. "I contacted everyone who has a studio at Sternberger. They all said they'd write a recommendation letter for me. I hope it works."

"Tomorrow I'll go by the UA office on my way to my studio and put in a good word for you, too. I know Connie personally," Jay said. "I don't see how she can resist when you have all those people pulling for you."

I couldn't help but feel hopeful, though I knew it was dangerous to do so. Would Connie resent the full court press on my behalf?

Samantha had been eating quietly throughout our discussion without saying a word. Finally, apparently satisfied that we'd exchanged all our news, she spoke up.

"I've made a decision," she said.

We both looked at her in surprise. Samantha hadn't been strong at making decisions, more content to go along with what others suggested.

"What is that, Sam?" Jay asked.

"I've decided what I want to do, but I need some help from you."

Jay and I looked at her expectantly. "So tell us," I said.

"Well," she said, fiddling with her fork nervously, "Brian might need some help when he gets out of the hospital. I called Guilford Tech this morning and found out they have a three-month nurses' aide program. I'd like to take the course and be ready to help when he comes home."

Jay and I looked at each other in astonishment. Neither of us had thought of the possibility Samantha could make a contribution. The more I thought about it, though, the more sense it made. It would give her a skill she could use anywhere, and it would ease the burden of Brian's care. In the event he came home with no ill effects after his stay at Shepherd Center, Samantha could get a job at any number of health facilities. She'd probably never make a lot of money, but it would give her a sense of self-worth and at least partially support her.

"Sam," Jay said, "what a wonderful, thoughtful thing for you to do. I believe you'd do well at Guilford Tech. You said you needed our help. I'll be happy to pay your tuition. I wouldn't be surprised, though, that you could get some kind of scholarship or financial aid."

"I already talked to them about that. And they told me they would have help for me. What I need you to do is teach me how to drive. And loan me enough money to buy a really cheap car." Samantha was gaining confidence now that Jay had approved of her idea. Her eyes shone brighter, and her voice wasn't nearly so hesitant.

"I can do better than that. Brian's old sedan isn't being used. I'll teach you to drive that, and you can use it till he's able to drive again. I don't think he'll need it before the end of your term. And maybe we could find you your own car by then."

My heart did a little flutter at his confidence that Brian *would* drive again.

Samantha jumped out of her chair and dashed around the table to hug Jay. "You are the best!" she exclaimed. Then she looked at me and threw me a kiss. "You too, Liz," she said. This was totally out of character for the Samantha I had known all these months.

That night as I lay in Jay's arms, I thought of all we had gone through in the past year and a half, all three of us. And it seemed that, although we still had mountains to climb, we were much closer to the top than we had been before.

# CHAPTER THIRTY-FIVE

It was December twenty-third, and Jay and I were standing on the enclosed porch off the living room at Sternberger Artists Center. We were waiting for our cue. I was wearing a dove gray suit that I'd had for many years but had little opportunity to wear. I'd splurged and bought a pretty silk blouse, but that was all that was new. I had my hair done at the hairdresser's for the first time in months, and I wore a gold locket that had belonged to Jay's mother. Inside was his baby picture at age three months. He had on new dark gray slacks and a guayabera, a shirt he'd bought in Mexico years earlier. His gray curls shone almost like a halo as the sunlight through the windows backlit his head. I thought he looked extraordinarily handsome.

We heard the chords of "The Power of Love" begin to play and stepped through the double door into the living room. The small solarium at the far end of the room was filled with white poinsettias banked under the windows on the tile shelves. A friend of Jay's who had a greenhouse lent them to us for the ceremony. A podium was placed in the center and Earl, Jay's friend who had a studio upstairs, stood before it. A licensed minister, he was pleased to be asked to conduct the ceremony.

Rows of chairs faced the podium with space for a center aisle. Rachel sat in the front row as well as Meredith and her new husband of five weeks, Carl. I met Carl shortly before their wedding when they eloped to the Bahamas, and I liked him very much. I thought he was a keeper. Meredith had finally realized she had been marrying for all the wrong reasons: money, looks, a good line. She chose men who swept her off her feet and once they got her, lost interest. Carl had far more substance than her other husbands.

Samantha and Brian sat beside them. Brian had been home for three weeks. He had come a very long way, but still needed therapy to improve his speech, balance, and gait. For now he wore a leg brace on his left side and his left hand was weak, but the doctors hoped it was temporary. He still went for therapy twice a week in Greensboro, and Samantha drove him there as he was not yet ready to get behind the wheel.

Samantha had completed her training at Guilford Tech just before Brian was discharged from Shepherd Center. I don't think I'd ever seen her so radiantly happy as the day of graduation ceremonies. I thought how much prettier she was when joy transformed her features. Jay and I took her to dinner at one of the nicest restaurants in town to celebrate. We normally couldn't afford such extravagance, but the occasion called for a one time budget buster.

Jay and I both were concerned how Brian would react when he came home to having Samantha as his caregiver. Although he could take care of most of his own needs, he still required help putting on the brace and dealing with things like buttons and shoe laces. She had been given instructions how to work with him on his speech, and they spent an hour or two a day with that.

Jay had told us after his first trip to visit Brian at Shepherd Center that his son was having problems dealing with outbursts and uncontrolled emotions. But with the support of his therapists he learned how to keep them under control, and by the time of his discharge, his attitude was better than I'd ever seen in him. His anger and resentment seemed to have faded. It was almost as if his accident had ultimately made him more resilient and less tense.

The rest of the chairs in the living room were filled with the artists and writers who had studios there and employees of the United Arts Council where I'd been working since September.

We walked arm-in-arm to the podium and Earl began, "We are gathered here today. . . ."

Ten minutes later Earl announced we were officially man and wife. Jay kissed me tenderly, and we turned to face our guests. They all stood and clapped, an unexpected but heart-warming response.

A table laden with food prepared by the Sternberger residents was set up in the large foyer. Rachel had taken charge of the refreshments, and the table was beautiful with a bouquet of white chrysanthemums mixed with red roses. There was a good rum punch, lovely little tea sandwiches, tiny cream puffs, chess tarts, and assorted nuts and mints.

It was a far cry from my elaborate first wedding and reception many years ago, but the simplicity spoke to where we were in our lives: blissfully happy with what we had, which wasn't much in the way of material possessions. We were secure in our love. All four of us were in a pretty good place with the future looking brighter. Brian was on the road to recovery; Samantha was happy in her own skin and had a skill that would serve her throughout her life. Jay was doing what he loved best which was to teach and paint, and I loved my job working with the artists and writers I cared for. I still had time for my own painting, and the three of us often spent Saturdays together in the studio out back working on our current projects. Even Brian was getting involved. As part of his occupational therapy, he chose to learn how to frame pictures. Jay had purchased the required equipment from a friend who was closing up his shop, and Brian had quite an eye for choosing the best mats and frames for each picture.

The guests mingled and ate, and we eventually moved the chairs out of the living room and played dance music.

Jay held me in his arms as we danced to the strains of "I Only Have Eyes For You." As we made our way slowly around the floor he leaned down and whispered in my ear, "Hello, Mrs. Kadlacek. I don't know about you, but if this is the first day of the rest of my life, I can hardly wait for day number two."

I laid my head on his shoulder, closed my eyes, and thought again how truly blessed I was to have this man, this second chance at life. "Me, too, Jay. And that goes for day number three and four and all the rest of them, ad infinitum."

# AUTHOR'S NOTE

The United Arts Council currently owns and operates the Sternberger Artists Center at 712 Summit Avenue in Greensboro. Built in 1926 by Sigmund Sternberger, the Center was donated in 1971 from the Sigmund Sternberger Foundation. Originally, the home housed the offices and member agencies of the United Arts Council. Today, the Sternberger Artists Center thrives with 90–100% occupancy with a variety of artists including writers, painters, photographers and more.

# ABOUT THE AUTHOR

**Nancy Gotter Gates** is the author of five mysteries in addition to her mainstream novel, *Sand Castles*. She's had thirty short stories published in various anthologies and literary magazines as well as dozens of poems. She lives in High Point, North Carolina, with her cat, Callie.